The Small Hours

The Small Hours

James Knight

Memories of a Kiss

First published by Cipher Books 2007

This edition published 2012

All texts and images © James Knight 2012

ISBN 978-1-4716-0859-9

jamesknight2012@gmail.com

Further copies of this book can be purchased online at
www.lulu.com

The Small Hours

Contents

Phantoms

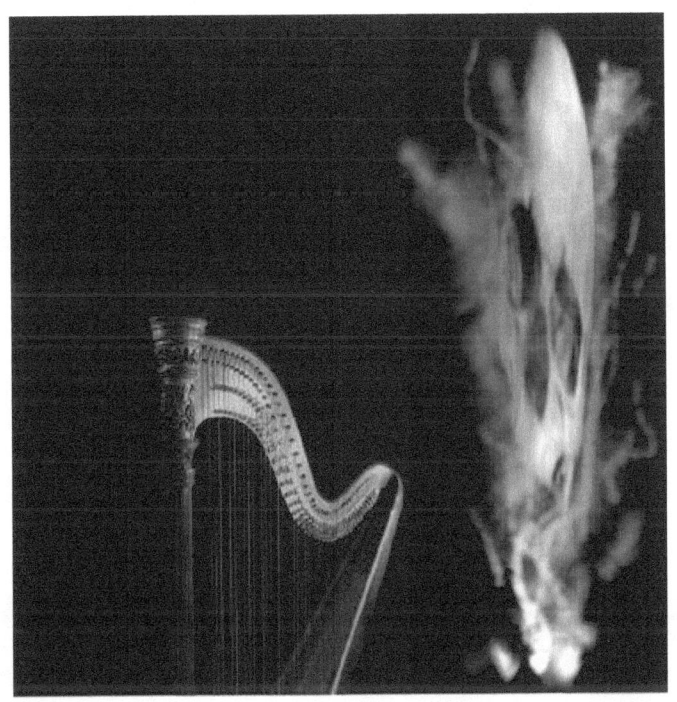

The Musician's Pact

Beginnings I

Begin with a blank page, then fill it with a blank landscape.

It all begins on these lonely sands. The sea is perfectly still; not a wave agitates its surface. It reflects a colourless, empty sky suffused with a faint and sourceless light. The horizon is a near-invisible silver band. No wind blows here, nothing stirs.

There is nothing but the beach, the sea and the sky, but something is waiting to exist.

The Beach

The beach was uninviting, but at least we could be alone here. She had insisted we come to this particular beach at just before sunrise, so that we could run along the deserted sands and jump into the grey waters and be alone, just the two of us, without fear of our fun being spoilt by other people. I had been sceptical and tired, but now I was glad we were here.

The beach descended from rocks and pebbles to a thin strip of sand licked by the quiet sea. The sky was still and dominated by cloud. There was no one here, just me and her and the cold pre-dawn light which greyed everything. It wasn't quite real, wasn't quite a dream. Looking out to the horizon I could almost forget the presence of the squat row of houses (most of them now just shells) and the promenade behind me.

She kissed me and suggested a swim in the sea. I didn't like the idea, particularly since it would mean taking off all of my clothes; what if someone were to turn up, jogging or walking his dog along the beach, and see me paddling naked? Looking into her eyes I blushed in anticipation of this possibility. Her face saddened momentarily, but then she let out a childish laugh and flung her clothes over the beach, one by one, so that they lay in a random sprawl on the wet sand. Then she ran into the sea and let it swallow her.

I gathered her clothes together and sat on a dry patch of sand. A faint yellow touched the clouds and the sea and a breeze caught the nape of my neck, making me tingle. I saw her blonde head bobbing in the placid waters as she breast-stroked to and fro. I waved and called out but she seemed absorbed in what she was doing. She gave to the simple act of swimming the same fierce concentration she gave to everything that mattered to her.

I closed my eyes and breathed deeply, filling my lungs with the cool salt breath of the sea.

When I opened my eyes the sun was rising from the sea and kissing the world with its first rays. She had swum much closer to the shore, and now she was standing up in the shallows and facing me, her naked wetness aflame with the sun, her eyes looking into my eyes, her hair tangled and moving.

Golgotha

In his dream Christ was a bloated corpse washed up on the beach. The crucifixion had taken place under water, before an audience of sharks and eels. Nameless creatures with bulbous eyes emerged from holes in rocks to witness the grand spectacle. The sacrificial victim made no attempt to free himself from the ropes binding his wrists and ankles, despite the fact that it was over a minute since he had taken his last breath. The lobsters (who had captured him and strapped him to the coral cross) were disappointed but not surprised by their prisoner's apathy, the waves having told them that he was not a man of action. As Christ drowned a man wearing a snorkel shot a harpoon into his side and luxurious clouds of black blood billowed about the wound. The sharks and eels sniffed closer. Seized by slow convulsions that wracked his body in waves, Christ closed his eyes forever.

It was at that moment that the Holy Ghost appeared, a monstrous octopus squirting jets of ink over the body of the drowned man.

The sun's first rays covered the beach and the dead man with a cold, grey light. For a moment the world seemed turned to stone. A dog sniffing at the contorted cadaver soon tired of the object of its scrutiny and padded off to its master, who lay asleep on a nearby bench, dreaming of love.

At Night the Mannequins Play Dead

a sea-front promenade of sticky ruin

    waving hands
        children's fearful laughter

    the sun's yoke sizzles across the stretched heat of
        the sky

    Mr Goitre and his clowns are back in town
        a greasepainted troupe of villains
    their show cut-price and cut-throat
    their eyes singing with mild madness
        roll up roll up
    see the smiles on darkened faces

    last year I went to the circus
    and wept after the grand finale

        sadder than the sea's slow swell and whisper

or Mr Whippy
            drowned
            washed up on the white waste
                mouth stupidly open eyes blind

  a breeze

    leather men with candyfloss smiles
        dodge behind arcades
            seeking little snakes

nothing to do now
never anything to do

waves break
in dismal droves

listen
the police sirens are sounding Mr Whippy's dirge

Tramp

you don't know what he's saying
and he isn't speaking to you anyway

rancid Elohim hatched him from shit and concrete
gave him eyes
etched signs on his shoes

he is king of a staggering catwalk
                drooling spirits
down alleys of fish smells and growls
he trails his mildewed mantle
joy and woe are woven fine
a clothing for the soul divine

he stops and sniffs the thick air
angels
                shifting in the sky's stained glass
are pissing in his coffee
                their smiles evaporating
he throws the warm white cup (soft as flesh)
to drench with this potion of life
the dead things, the never-alive things

which bloom   pregnant with shadow

a cur blurts its loony caw-caw

the sun intervenes

enraged
and the tramp sees
luciferous
the dry white god
the god of cleanliness and geometric death strategies
passing in a skull on wheels

whiter than white

Brassaï in Paris

Unknown Paris of delightful terrors

Unseen Paris of waste and rain

Paris of marionettes

Paris of iron dawns and dead streets

Paris weeping at twilight

Paris of corsets and limbs in windows and in minds

Paris of faceless men making signs across distances

Naked Paris

Paris of whores in the crying light

Paris of banal offerings

Of flesh of thighs of tits

Paris sweating through the close night

Paris stooping to put on her stockings

The anonymous customer scratching his arse

Paris of fleas of lice of rats of stale beer of dust

Buxom Paris stretching on a soiled divan

Whispering Paris

Paris of stark trees in the fog

Stark trees in the cold fog and light coming from
    nowhere

Light coming from the hotel sign

Floating frozen

Paris of lonely benches and sleeping men

Paris of the solitary wanderer stopping to gaze with
    eyes of blind desire at posters advertising health
    and wealth

Paris of the empty boulevard

Paris of a phantom Seine and bridges bridges bridges

Criminal docks and towpaths

Paris perpetually dark perpetually autumnal

Paris of cafés where sharpfaced young men lean

    towards their darlings their eyes whetted on the

    sharp mirrors their hands not visible for now

Of cafés where smoking drudgery lifts a glass of beer

    to her cynical lips

Of cafés where eyes converge on the happy couple

Your eyes your uninvited eyes

Paris of voyeurs

Paris of look-but-don't-touch

Paris of inscrutable tableaux

Paris of signs

Paris of hieroglyphs

Secret signals riddled throughout the streets

Paris of graffiti of accumulations

Paris a text forever being written a painting never

    finished

Paris a woman applying fresh makeup while a man

    waits on the other side of

        the screen

The spectral city smiling at midnight

Full of love

Paris kissing the moon

Vampire

five a.m.

a pencilled skyline of factories and houses
      squats
under the belly of the clouds

fractured laughter under the railway bridge
where three vagrants are dancing round a fire of
   refuse
a fourth thumping a maudlin tune
from a child's xylophone

the air
      heavy with rust and dust
      hangs uneasily
        over
collapsed walls of corrugated iron
            sleeplessness

shadows under a stark tree
    twisting like roots
      conspiring whispers

one of the dancers has slipped over and cut his
   forehead
the xylophone still shows its sharp little teeth
a modest fork of blood accumulates dirt on its descent

a scrawny urban cat
bristles and flees

the hourly fast train passes

like a thick poison
        dawn seeps
                through the crack of the skyline

Moth

the madman rants

the madman spits

the madman stares lunacy of eyes destroyed by black
    fires

      numberless names in the filth of his palm

the madman sighs

      banal futile

the madman condemns everything in himself and out
        of himself

      everything young and clean and moneyed

the madman is a moth

  a dirty brown moth

      burning its paper wings

      too enamoured of fire

      too giddy around light

      wheeling reeling

  a dusty grey moth

  flattened to ashes under your hand

  no blood no ooze of life

  just dust

and you wash your reasonable sane hands

you who stare every waking morning into a mirror into
      a skull

you who lick the coin and kiss the plastic

you who shake fists at the surprise of sunrise

you who submit to the black screen the blank screen

                  screaming
you who sit and wait
          as a madman sits and waits
          in the pity of morning
you who rise and retire and rise and expire
you who can do nothing
          as the madman does nothing
          - everything is full of eyes knives threats -
you who make a living of dying
you who make a killing
you who hunt the stone cities
you who lust in secret your hand not daring to graze
          her skirt your eyes averted from hers
you who drink and fall down and laugh and piss
               yourself
you who point at folly and children and pictures
you who sleep savagely in the arrears of dream

and outside now the madman sobs his heart of
magnets of flies
          his unanswerable lament
          his blistering doggerel
the madman sobs
and in his bruised fist
the scraps the dog-ears the fag-ends the dust the shit
the fire-crisped papery moth
poem of melancholy song of death
he has crushed 'twixt finger and thumb

Homage to Pierre Reverdy

I

When the windows melted

and space became conspicuous

you sat in a haze of absence

your eyes projecting

  a web

   a wall

formal inner constructions

   succinct geometric

       explosions

articulating enigma

II

All the clocks are striking at once

and a lizard blinks

  its ineffable breath

  the space between words

  space tight or pregnant

  space living grave

gaunt forms gathering

fleshed with shadow

all within your fractured gaze

stopping at the wall

the eyelid forever closed

to the shifting vistas

of vague paradises

   a high and tactile

   stench of rot

(you were never drunk on paradise)

III

Last week your animals

were a finger of fur

in a sparse landscape

a clawed toothed silent

facet of your

inscrutable design

today they are dissolving

  yet the long wall remains

the solid line shadow heavier than eyes

dazzled by the light of duress.

Beginnings II

Begin with a blank page, then fill it with an imaginary landscape.

It all begins on these sands strewn with black debris and the patterns of seashells. The sea is an ocean of blood, almost still, the faintest waves agitating its surface. It reflects a sunset sky and a fixed body of cloud. The horizon is a near-invisible silver band. Nothing stirs but the whispering west wind.

Nothing exists but what you can see and feel and hear, but something is waiting to exist, struggling to find form in the naked clouds.

The Song of the Clowns

Mr Goitre sits in the sizzling light, amazed at the pie flying towards his face from the hand of Mr Hernia.

***

Dishevella is a dirty slut of a clown. She sits in doorways in her torn stockings and smeared makeup, laughing obscenely at passersby. Sometimes, when business is slack, she stands in the middle of the pavement and pirouettes on her left foot, mechanically, clumsily, like a toy in need of repair. But you should see the smile cracking across her face!

***

The dressing room is a scene of carnage: noses, red and swollen, lie on the floor; someone's lunatic face stares up from the table; enormous gloved hands crawl over chairs and torn costumes. In the mirror, threaded with cracks, is the appalling spectre of Mr Goitre's head and torso, naked, white, fractured, slashed with red, knotted, pimpled, a dead chicken!

***

Mr Garrotte screams with laughter while his masked assistants set fire to Mr Hernia.

***

As the lights go down Dishevella is left alone in the arena, clasping a rag doll to her crimson heart. The doll's head lolls mournfully to one side. Lights out. Ferocious applause.

***

Messrs Goitre, Hernia and Garrotte are battling it out in the arena over the affections of the lovely but dissolute Dishevella. Mr Goitre is armed with an enormous hammer, which he swings about with drunken panache. Mr Hernia's fists, monstrous and red, beat the air and the persons of any who get too near to him (with the exception of the beautiful Dishevella). Mr Garrotte is unarmed but he moves with remarkable agility for one so rotund, jumping over canons and bodies, ducking and scampering away from the attacks of the other males. Occasionally he succeeds in striking an antagonist with the heel of his silly, oversized shoe, in a lightning movement like the kick of a donkey. And amidst the noise and violence, Dishevella becomes ever more aroused by the sight and thought of these virile specimens fighting over her body. Whenever one of the combatants gets close to her she encourages him with a pout and a pantomime wink, whilst picturing him bouncing up and down on top of her. She does not have a favourite, though the size of Mr Goitre's hammer gives her something to think about. But ultimately she must accept whoever wins the battle. Last night it was Mr Hernia, and the night before it was Mr Goitre. The night before that... but it is no good, she cannot remember that far back. So she executes her robotic Salomé dance and waits for the end of the act.

***

Mr Hernia cannot even walk across the arena without stumbling, tripping, falling flat on his contorted face. The apparently simple business of getting from one place to another is not so straightforward, after all.

***

Mr Garrotte has been wedged into the barrel of the canon. Only his head is clear of this terrible gun. He weeps and screams and begs mercy of the naughty Dishevella, who affects not to hear him and bends over very ostentatiously to light the fuse, wiggling her swollen rump in the air for the benefit of the dads in the audience. Then, still bent forward, she creeps backwards, away from the canon. The thick fuse wire hisses and throws off sparks, shrinking with the rapidity of the collective heartbeat of the audience. The arena falls silent, save for the sibilance of the burning wire and the strangulated pleas of Mr Garrotte. Mr Mort, the Circus Master, has even instructed his cringing minions that there should, on this occasion, be no drumroll to build up the tension, as it is quite clearly not needed. The world waits. Mr Hernia is perfectly still, for the first time this evening. The fuse has almost completely burnt down. Dishevella puts her hands over her ears and somehow raises her behind even further in the air. Mr Goitre, waiting to go on after Mr Garrotte's body has described an elegant parabola over the circus ring, is suddenly aware of the silence, and he closes his eyes and waits. Mr Garrotte too closes his eyes and stifles his tears. The fizzing fuse runs out. The last spark. And nothing. Nothing happens! Several seconds go by, and still no explosion, still Mr Garrotte is stuck in the canon. Dishevella straightens up, disappointed. People in the audience start mumbling and giggling. Messrs Hernia and Goitre breathe out, shrug and get ready for the next act. Mr Mort shakes his great leaden head. And in the barrel of the canon, Mr Garrotte opens his eyes and starts laughing, like a man set free, like a child, like a delirious victor, like a baboon, like a madman.

***

Broken bottles, spilled beer, overturned chairs, a smashed table. Dishevella and Mr Goitre sit on the floor, legs and backs straight like wooden toys, heads slumped forward. Dishevella giggles to herself, with the puny, fairy-like voice of a little girl. Mr Goitre snores and mumbles, erupting occasionally into belligerent glossolalia and then, still asleep, subsiding into relative quiet. Upright against the wooden door, his lurid green suit pinned to it by several large throwing knives, is Mr Hernia, whose head, like those of Dishevella and Mr Goitre, is also slumped forward on his breast. Unlike the two on the floor, however, Mr Hernia makes no sound. A little drop of blood trickles out of the corner of his bloated mouth and runs down the greasepaint.

***

Mr Mort, the Circus Master, wears a black suit and never smiles. He avoids sunlight, and is often to be found sitting in his caravan, sipping scotch. He has fifteen murders to his name, eight of these being his own clowns. He is a man easily disappointed. Loved to excess as a child by a mother maniacally maternal, he now styles himself as a modern Timon, cultivating his misanthropy with graceful detachment. He reads a lot of Baudelaire and regards himself as a *poete maudit*, his tormented strophes the colourful spectacles he offers to the moronic masses, his exquisite alexandrines the polish and glitz of the show.

***

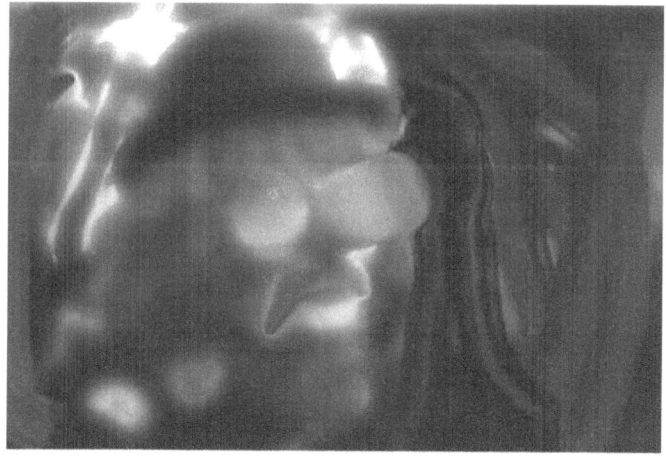

Mr Goitre sits naked in his dressing room, staring at his reflection in the cracked mirror.

***

To crazy music, Mr Hernia dashes about the circus ring, throwing bouquets of flowers from his tiny bowler hat to the outstretched hands of women and children in the audience. As he runs around his nose gets bigger and bigger, until it is so large that he is forced to beckon over the masked assistants and ask them to carry it before him. More flowers, more colours, more scents, more enchanted women and children. And the nose gets bigger, a monstrous embryo, a sack of blood and madness, a red planet.

***

Fully wound up, arms and legs twitching on the ends of strings, eyes agog and unseeing, body polygonally rendered and realistically textured, waiting for the hand that will flip the red switch, springtensed and panting, his big red tongue flopping listlessly out of his painted mouth, Mr Garrotte sits cross-legged in the centre of the abandoned circus ring, desperately lonely, desperately unhappy.

***

In his dressing room, before the cracked mirror, Mr Goitre's swollen hands grope Dishevella's breasts, thighs, neck. Fat fingers trace trails in the greasepaint sweating over her face. Malevolent eyes stare into the mirror.

***

In an alleyway on the outskirts of town, a good two miles from the circus, Dishevella is dancing for Mr Hernia. He is sitting on a dustbin, hands in pockets, fag in mouth, watching her stilted twirls, her automaton arabesques. Pirouetting, she laughs the heartily filthy laugh of the jaded and degraded. Mr Hernia could

29

watch her for hours. For once he has no desire to fuck her. It is enough for him to see her body move in this extraordinary way. He sits enchanted by his favourite toy.

***

For Mr Mort, violence is an art form. So when he smashes a bottle in the face of one of the masked assistants, or throws Mr Garrotte into a vat of sulphuric acid, or disembowels Dishevella, he does it knowing that he is the artist and the victims his materials. He does not expect anyone else to understand this.

***

Mr Garrotte has malfunctioned. Mr Hernia has him bent over the dressing room table, and is trying to rewire him. He pulls out handfuls of red wires, blue wires, green wires, yellow wires, black wires, uninsulated wires (if only he had some rubber gloves!), thick wires, thin wires, stiff wires, flexible wires, coiled wires, straight wires, wires attached to nothing, spaghetti wires, worm wires, snake wires, live wires, dead wires, string wires, silk wires, gossamer wires, tough wires, gentle wires, loving wires, sensuous wires, insinuating wires, hateful wires, despairing wires, hopeless wires, faithless wires, reams and reams of them, reams and reams and reams of unhappy, entangled wires.

***

Dishevella cannot even talk to Mr Mort, the Circus Master, without stumbling on her words, tripping, falling flat. The apparently simple business of communicating something to someone is not so straightforward, after all.

***

In the mirror, as before, the fractured torso and head of the melancholy clown.

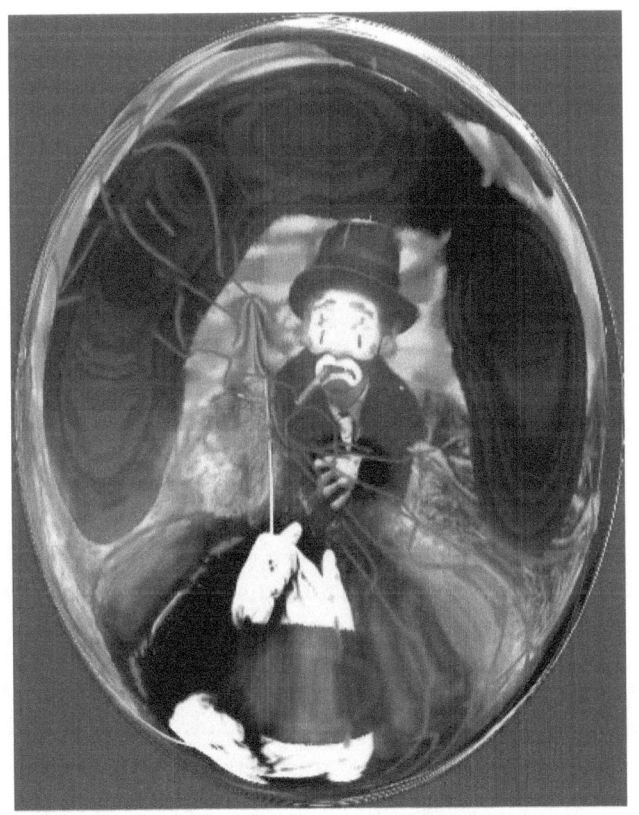

The Carcass

The final form Venus took was that of a beautiful red carcass hanging in a butcher's shop window. Her crucified limbs twitched with the joy of the meathook and her splayed ribcage offered itself, an open shell, to whoever passed in front of that grimy backstreet window. The black skies melted into rain on the passersby, driving them ever more furiously past Venus' window, but still they found time to incline an eye towards her splendid rawness. One man, a lonely old soul, stopped in his tracks and stared without blushing straight into her. She could feel the strength of his desire through the glass partition. She was the princess of the ball, the prom queen, the ravishing courtesan! The butcher's shop had become a theatre and she was the leading lady, elevated above an audience that (for now) demanded no action, just the simple pleasure of looking and longing.

But it wasn't all perfect. Martin, the butcher's son, was a horrible young man. Whenever his father was occupied at the back of the shop he would take a big knife and score a line in Venus' back, causing her unspeakable pain. He didn't know why he did it; he just couldn't help himself. Poor Venus felt like a defenceless old lady when Martin attacked her, and hourly she counted her gashes with the trembling of a woman who knows the greatest violation is yet to come.

Mad Uncle

my uncle lives in shadows, talks to strangers

he won't honour the promises of clocks
or the vicissitudes of daylight

he cuts the throats of unwelcome dreams

once [when he still had choice in these matters]
he allowed a pigeon into his lounge
just to see how it would cope with tea and platitudes

he then realised he could provide neither
so another experiment was shelved

my uncle has teeth jagged as the summit of the forest
and as black

which he plunges into necks of lamb

cool of morning, meat of evening

when the jaded moon circumvents the possible
he's there growling at phantoms
ten dead birds blighting his forehead

Girls Outside a London Nightclub

congregating about the black glass doors

the painted females with their perfumes

offer legs spectral under stockings

to the passersby

and their dreams

cigarettes and blondness like smoking guns

a skirt reminiscent of a fuchsia

waiting for rain

the superficial smartness of three thugs in suits

faces dead ahead, arms rigid

as the next carload rolls lingeringly past

it's impossible not to look at the girls

every fixed eyelash, every curved nonchalance

swells in dimmed eyes

in eyes forgetful of what they might have seen

in eyes like fairground mirrors

in eyes forever searching for food

in devouring eyes

in dissolving eyes

in eyes wheels headlights rear-view mirrors

in eyes not receiving but projecting

what fleshy silhouettes on what blank screens

fractured assemblages of breasts and hips

pulsating in strobes

these girls don't merely exist
these girls exude themselves
into the air
soft halos more than a trick of the electric light
coming from behind them
come and taste
lips tasting of sugar
lips tasting of blood
half-articulate promises in vapour pouring from those
lips
echoing bittersweet nothings, melancholy neon
we all get hurt by love and we all have a cross to bear
those lips seem to burn

from somewhere not far away
unseen animals lick the moon
tarnished near-round mirror
with their cries

the whole night seems ready to burn

Landscape with Bones

the cactoid vastness of a living desert
flattened under the sun

bones, the cleanliness of death,
leave the filigree vultures hungry

you drove through,
your wheels launching an ecstasy of sand
      dusty dirigibles
appeasing your taste for the picturesque

the landscape yielded to your imperious glances,
remodelled its dunes,

                      hatched oases;
a skeleton broke into a panicked gallop,
as if a predator more romantic than starvation hunted
    here

in writing, I mimic you:
things, essences reduce to order,
dead buffaloes please the eye,
everything is sentient and alive,
the sand is a parched monster
and lizards are signs
referring solely to us

wonder at the conjuror!

he can squeeze not just reds

      but blues and greens

            from the obliging Coccus cacti

~~ground zero~~

going to see Ground Zero

gawpers at the spectre

sightseers of nothing

yeah, then we went to look at something that wasn't

    there

it was very moving I got a great shot

and he snaps at the air

while a grinning woman from Japan

scans with breezy camcorder

    the scene

most New Yorkers don't want

a new building on the site

where the brave brothers fell

the phantom edifice of the Twin Towers

forever collapsing forever pristine

two towers, one image

blocking out space, heavily felt

its absence a presence

a chunk out of skyline

(newsmen must feed)

a gap, a taboo, flesh made word

stone made breath

sacred vacancy

two empty columns streaming with newsprint

invisible monument to war and terror

unreal symbol of defiance, victory, defeat, a nation's

   heart, the cry of the oppressed, the biggest

   moment of our lives

silently conspiring with Bush Bin Laden

weeping in Manhattan's insomnia

the Twin Towers never existed

save as models of destruction

pouting posing for the press

Ground Zero

   language of fire and stone

   a virtual spurt of divine blood

   Golgotha on the TV news

let's move over there honey

I wanna see some more

this ruinous poem

Beginnings III

A blank page soon fills with black words.

It all begins on these sands strewn with debris and fragments of seashells. The sea is an ocean of blood, almost still, the faintest waves agitating its surface. It reflects and magnifies a sunset sky and a hanging body of cloud. The horizon is a garrotting wire. Nothing stirs but a clot of shadows on the derelict pier.

At first it seems that nothing else exists here, but far out to sea is the silhouette of a yacht, motionless on the red water; and a phantom moon is beginning to materialise.

The Corpse

The blade of the half-moon hangs over black water. Slow, heavy waves carry a precious cargo in the direction of the ruinous shore.

The cargo is a drowned film star whose celebrity had made her the prey of a sinister group of men. They enacted their secret ritual at sea, then cast her naked into the water. Ravished by formless creatures shooting up from the depths at the promise of her touch, she drifts with hair that has become seaweed and limbs that have become tentacles. The pretty celluloid smile persists on lips turning to coral.

Dawn approaches as the shore approaches. The grey beaches are deserted and behind them loom the collapsed buildings and scaffolds. Seagulls regard with carrion eyes the twisted wreck of flesh rolling towards the shore.

As the sun rises the sea disgorges the murdered woman. She lies spreadeagled on the sand. Her lips offer themselves, an open shell, to the indifference of shingle and driftwood. The sun ignites her wetness with treacherous kisses.

An hour later a lone man walking his dog along the beach comes across the corpse. He looks about him, then gathers the dead woman lovingly in his arms and makes his way swiftly back the way he came.

Lava

One Word and All is Lost

Rant

rain falls on 10 Downing Street end of another general
        election victory
the third in a row for Tony Blair and sulphurous
      advisors rubbing hands in the background
how did this happen?
this wannabe statesman heavy with dollars and suits
this wannabe everyman
look, I'm just a guy, like you
I feel the hand of History on my shoulder
this have-it-both-ways salesman of words and
      groomed smiles
this take-it-anyway empty-eyed vessel
who can't even dream
can't even come to life
limbs stiff with rigour of mortarshells
raining on Baghdad in someone else's dream
raining blood
bodies leaking oil in dismal sun-blasted streets
how did this happen?
this man of tight smiles and tough choices
crooning Beatles numbers to oriental admirers
this man who sends reality spinning
we see the colours the blurred patterns the ghost of a
     form
but nothing stays fixed the eye doesn't rest
shapes don't emerge
just the spinning the spinning
the rictus broadens

sooner or later we forget stillness
we forget patterns and meanings
we switch over to the other side
hurry up, Big Brother's starting!

Body

the body exploded

flowerlike

how can I put this

open

yielded

innards outwards

petals of lungs

thorns of ribs

how else to say it

bloom of blood

teeth seeds

burgeoned bludgeoned

that's it, it isn't anything other than this

open burning in the sun

heliotropic

lung-petals and teeth-seeds

thorn-ribs

and I the bee

burying myself in this

as I have described

drunk on the honey of blood

Bells shatter...

Bells shatter in my head

trees falling

I call your name
all of your names
hundreds of them

The wind slips its head into the noose of your
imaginings

Nightmares

first this clock hammer rapping on my skull
tall as a scream

       the bedroom mists over in her dolly eyes

someone outside whispers
     love or consolation
         an empty kiss

              her breasts under the coil of suns

why don't you just fuck off
the simplest gestures grow
    clownlike

and burst with seed of song

keep playing your demented nocturnes,
Mr Scriabin

     let the cars' teeth tease you

Improvisation 1

hind legs disappearing

the well

a night resounding with bells

the last train leaving before it was due

her smile erasing itself her eyes turning away

these little moments of departure

moments of no consequence

nothing follows

Improvisation 12

let me go said the little voice witchlike unlike anything
    I'd heard
let me go let me go it repeated I didn't know what to
    do
whether let it out what was it or keep it in
was I hurting it was it me I didn't know
let me out it insisted most peevishly I thought
so I didn't let it out I kept it in
and after a few days of evermore feeble pleading
it died

Improvisation 15

and then other voices started up some of them
   whispering some growling
they all seemed to be demanding things it was difficult
   to tell what
how dare they invade me like this but what did they
   care
I was just a vessel or receptacle or yawning abyss for
   them to spin around in
the problem was amidst all their noise I couldn't hear
   myself think
or when I thought I could it turned out to be one of
   their voices not mine
an alien voice not unlike mine but subtly different
   articulating ideas I abhor
this was most annoying still I strained to hear myself
   think but without success
the voices were too loud or too many or perhaps I had
   ceased to think and had not realised

Mirror

False Perspective

Daddy Short-legs

Little Voice's daddy eats horses, carrots, prayers and
promises
his teeth glint in the blood of dawn
his gut rumbles with the cries of naughty little boys

Evenings go quickly
no one stirs from under him
except my eye my poor little eye

Little Voice dreams and plots
stacks up the guns that'll blow dad away

First Sadness

Little Voice felt sadness for the first time
it oozed from under the mattress
and coiled about his feet

It seemed to him that the world was in mourning

Won't someone nail my hands to the headboard, he
       thought,
give me what I have earned

But in truth he'd done nothing

Nothing, just the ticking of the clock
and the yellowing of his feet

Lights Out

Tormented by strange dreams, he shook and sweated on his bed. The light had gone from his eyes long ago and most people, when they met him in the street or in one of the local shops, assumed that he was dead. Birds nested in his ears and mouth. You couldn't talk to him about anything, he just never listened. His whole life revolved around the downward spiral of nightmares that opened at his feet every time the sun went down. He suffered from vertigo and once fell down five flights of stairs because he had made the mistake of looking down the stairwell. He was always teetering on the edge of one crisis or another, and if it wasn't his own inner strife it was something to do with the habit he had acquired of murdering people, usually attractive women, and usually by pushing them out of a window or off a ledge or down some stairs. The fall through space of a beautiful young woman had for him the quality of a religious ceremony, over which he was the officiating priest. The victim became a scapegoat, suffering the punishment he felt was really owed to him. He had no doubt in his mind that his terrible attacks of vertigo were an indication from a higher power that he deserved a fatal fall himself, as penance for some obscure transgression committed in his sleep. For his dreams were always bad and in them he would invariably carry out unspeakable acts of violence and perversion, whilst another part of him looked on sickened and aghast. What the poor man failed to realise was that his dreams constituted the very punishment he feared, and it was therefore quite unnecessary for him to go to the trouble and inconvenience of pushing all those women to their deaths. But there was nobody in his life to point this out to him.

[ink]

world of ink
ink skies ink land

I take the train in
I barely remember my name

the ink seeps into me

Blood

spring
   revolving in space

a skull

hot blood the sap rising
gunsmoke convolutions
                      spirals ascending
     to form
            this mirthful mindless head

black magic of the seasons

I watch you undressing
you are older now
your bones show through

      you paint a double helix in my blood
        I am lost in it

Worm

I've got this hideous idea that there's a nest of tapeworms in my gut. They're quite young and very small, and the only sign of their presence is an occasional day-long itching of the anus.

I suppose sooner or later there won't be enough food to go round and they'll devour each other until only one is left, fatly triumphant. This king worm will then stretch along the corridors of my intestines and feed, feed, feed! Eventually I'll be losing weight so fast that I can no longer ignore the problem.

How the hell will the doctors be able to get it out of me?

That grizzled king worm! Living in me like a foetus!

Me-Poem I

Refracted, distracted, disguised, surprised
chasing my own tail
chasing someone else's tail
or is it a rope?
hunched, bunched
up inside this knot of entrails
this knot of me
not of me
digesting the inedible world
(indelible word)
sick to the stomach
giddy and gorged
undone overdone

silent

Me-Poem II

idea of me:
brittle coil
in wombsoup
- an alien!

Reflections

"A whole network of grimaces and contortions opposes the raft of his age returning to the secret springs of his heart."
André Breton & Paul Eluard

At soft and pink time the biggest shapes moved and

     jabbered

while my arms and legs wrestled my brain for control.

At white time, stretches of crystalline forms dissolving,

     regrouping,

a voice browner and stiffer than the rest reverberated

     in the cupboard.

I assimilated everything in the room, every nuance and

     nuisance,

drank it, made it me.

          And yet, all the liquid I

so meekly let in

escaped. I cried.

At blue time I roamed creation, I was a monarch,

killing shadows with my stare.

At carmine time curvaceous paleness

     streaked the air

        with scent and songs

and I couldn't move.

(Did I have a rival king?
Was he the lean of the walls or
the noise coming from under
the stairs?)

At yellow time I feasted on the following :
the eyes of my captors,
the bones of the rival king's emissaries,
the flesh of giants,
the reds, the blues,
the thoughts of everyone,
my adventures.
It was all too much, the plate was full, it was always
full, no matter how much I threw at my face it was full,
friendly voices out of sight turned threatening,   the
rain beginning,   the   television laughed and
trumpeted vague sorrows, I still couldn't get through
this terrain of orange and brown, the noises from
under the stairs were distracting, where was the rival
king in all this?

At grey time I stink in my mausoleum,
prey to mouths full of forks and words.
My brain has beaten my arms and legs
in the battle for control.

A Beach

The sea is a sheet of copper

hammered by the evening sky

Seagulls

    flickers of sperm

are mirrored by the spume

        surging into the open legs of the beach

The sky

    inflicts blow upon blow

I walk down to the pebbles

Bulbous rocks are the rumps the breasts the heads of

        lovers

I don't see myself amongst them

People have left the slough of their real selves down

here

    condoms

    bottles cans syringes

    a bikini top

The febrile cries

    of gulls

        seem to name them

Further down

the sand is inviting

Soft shapes appear

as I let the sea heave onto my shoes.

Microcosmos

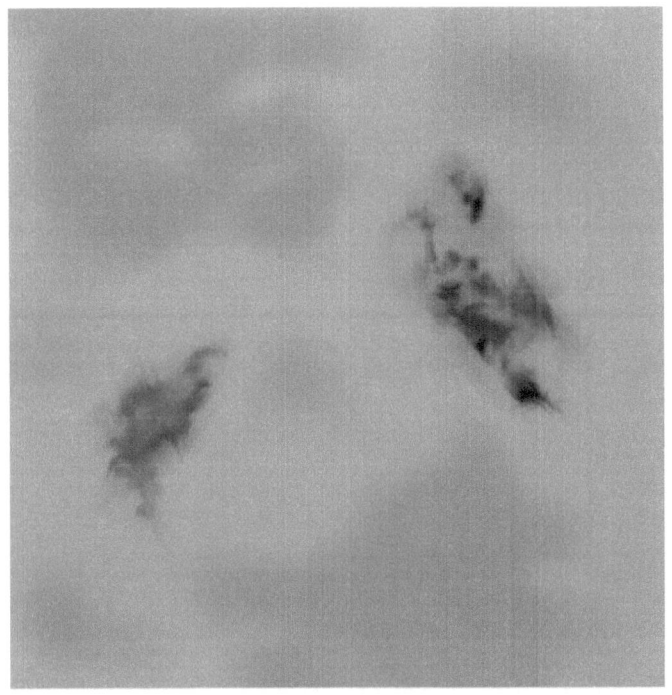

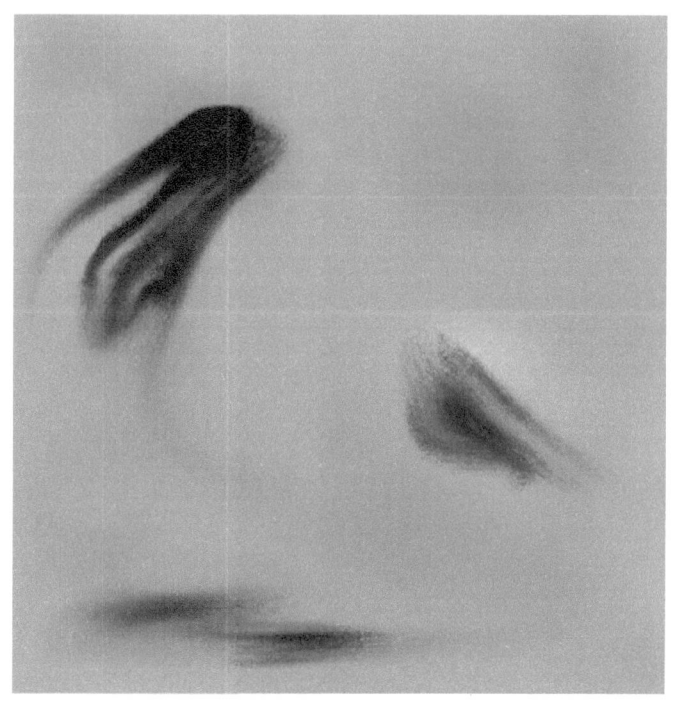

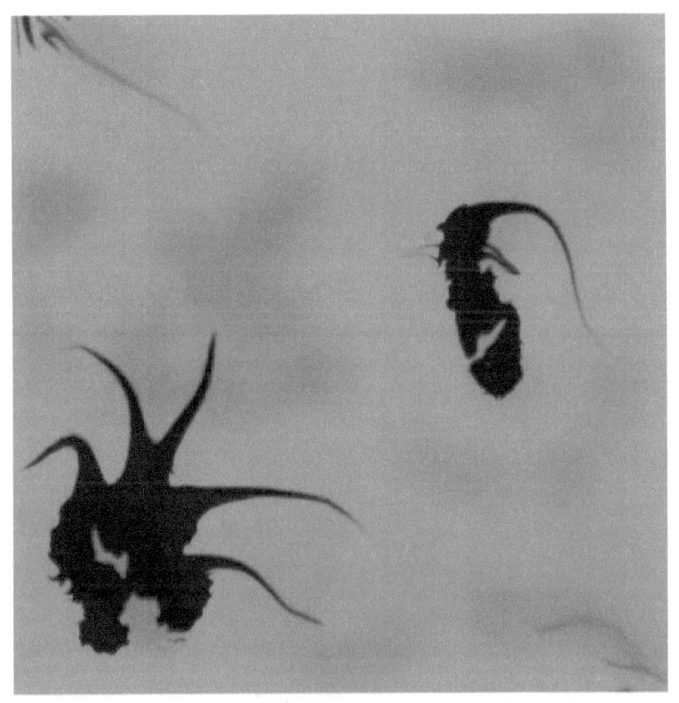

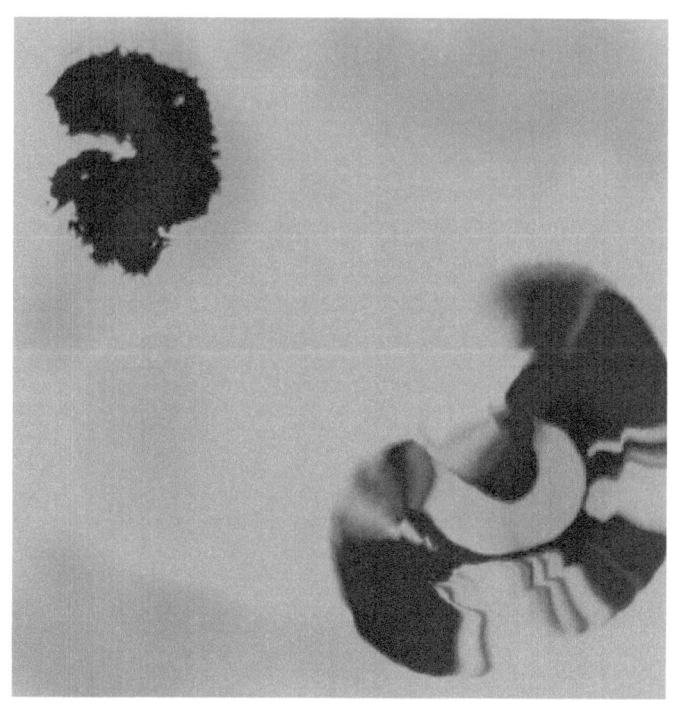

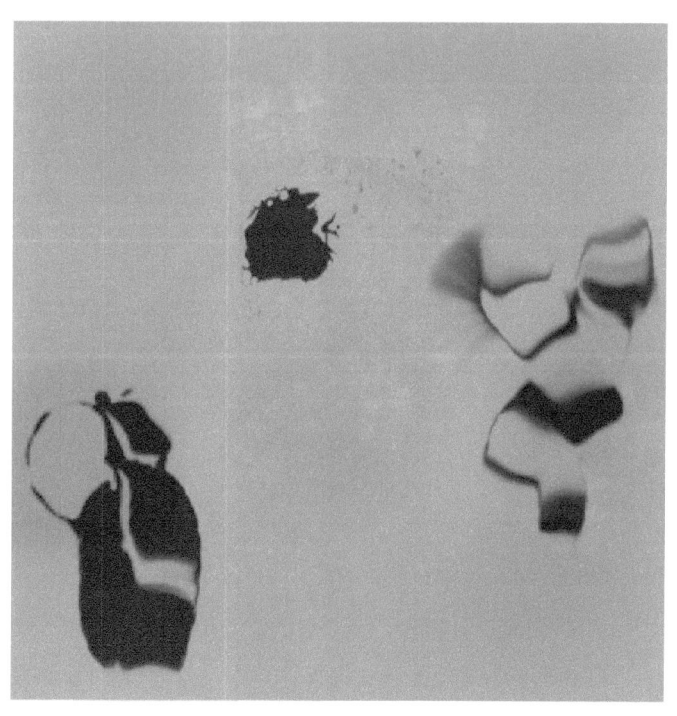

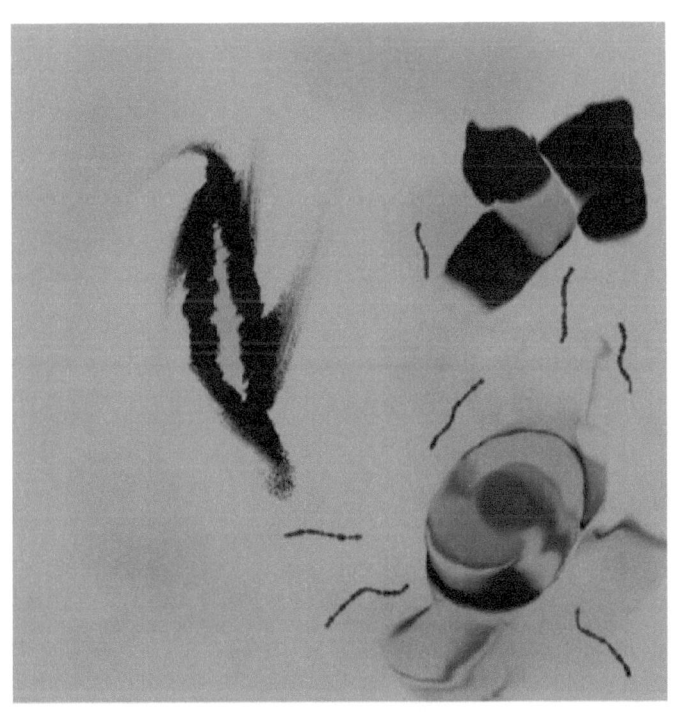

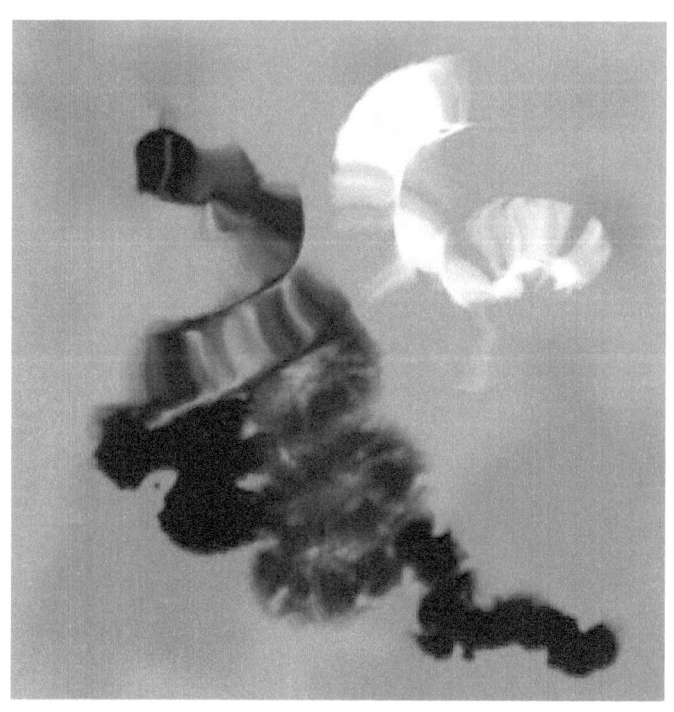

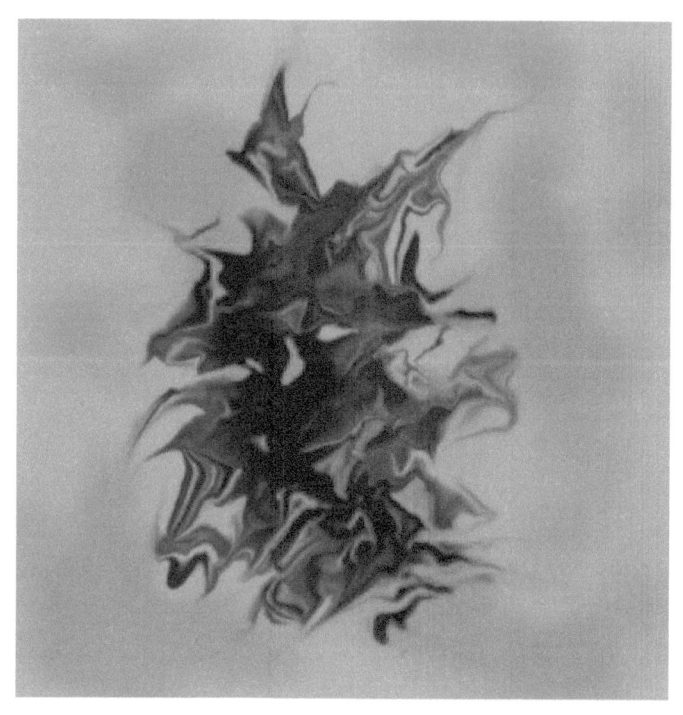

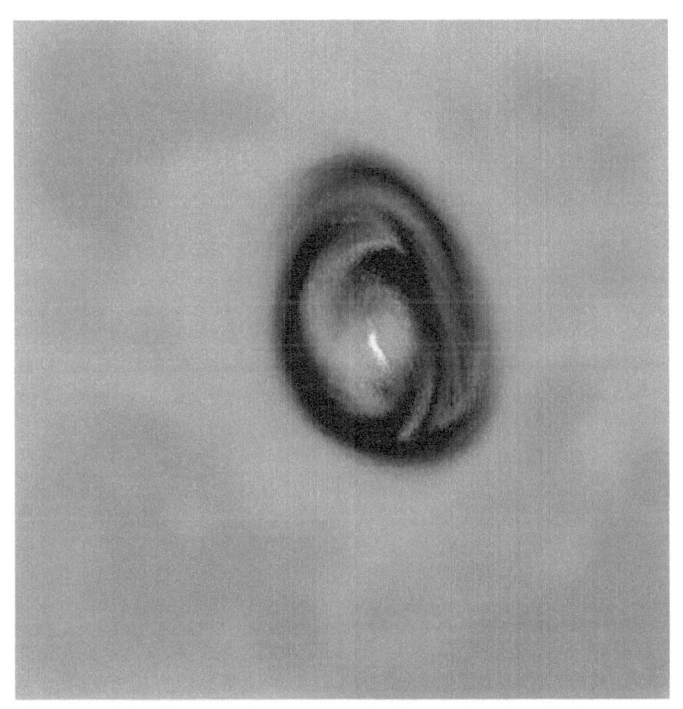

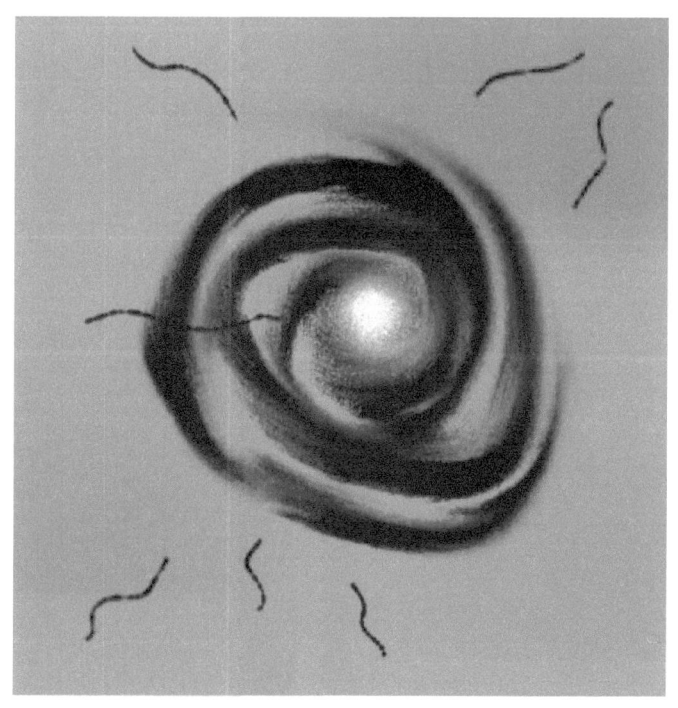

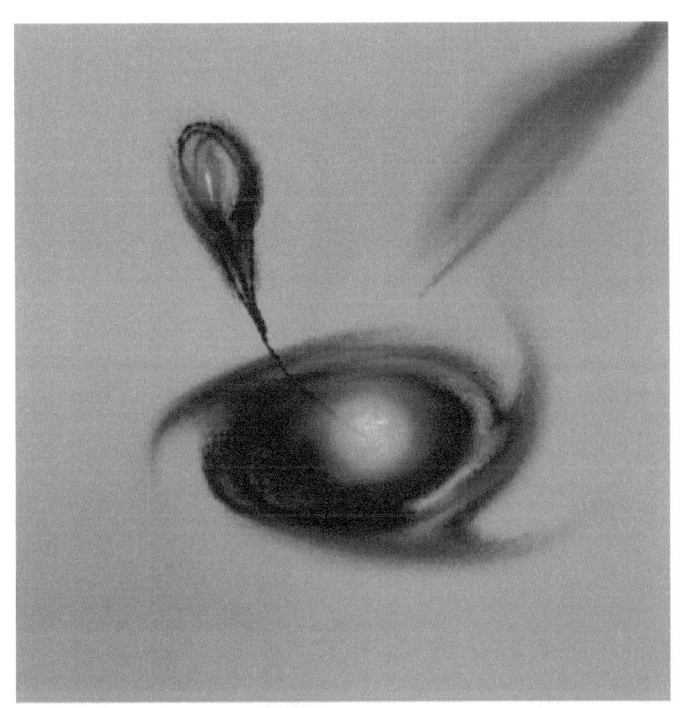

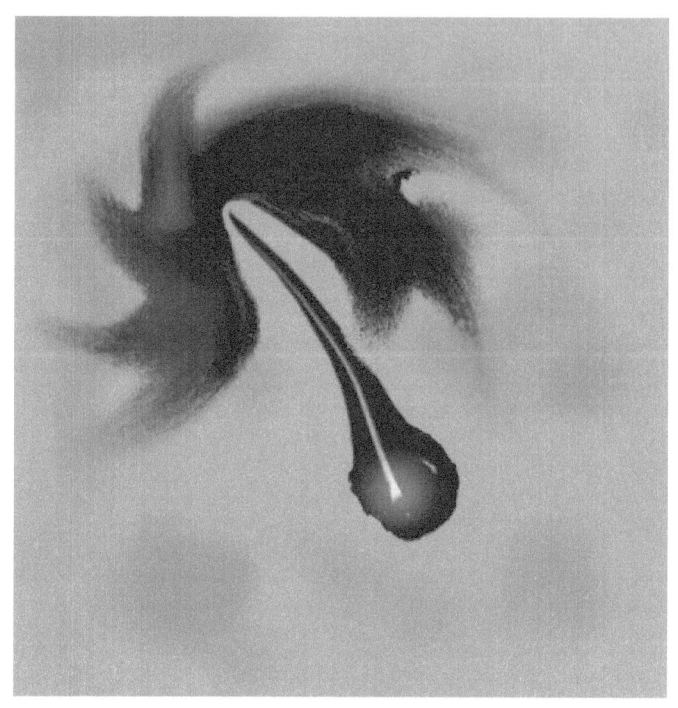

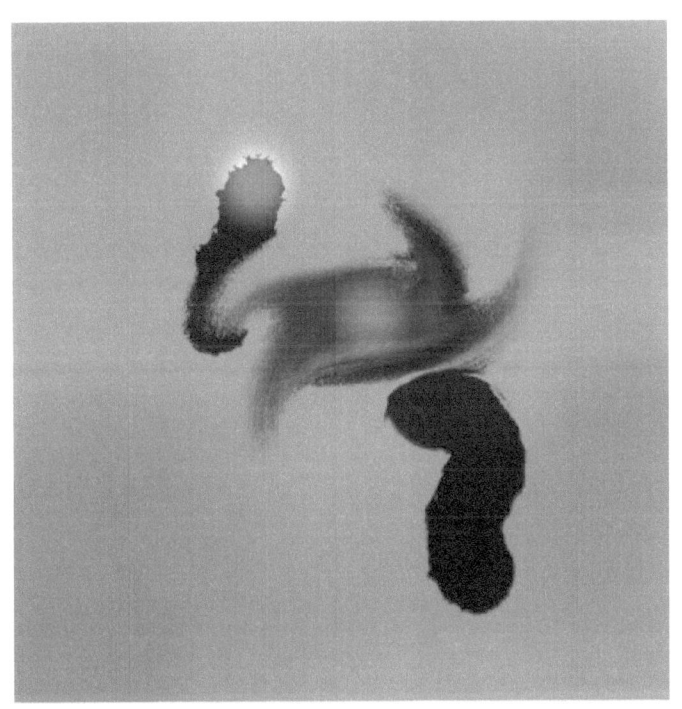

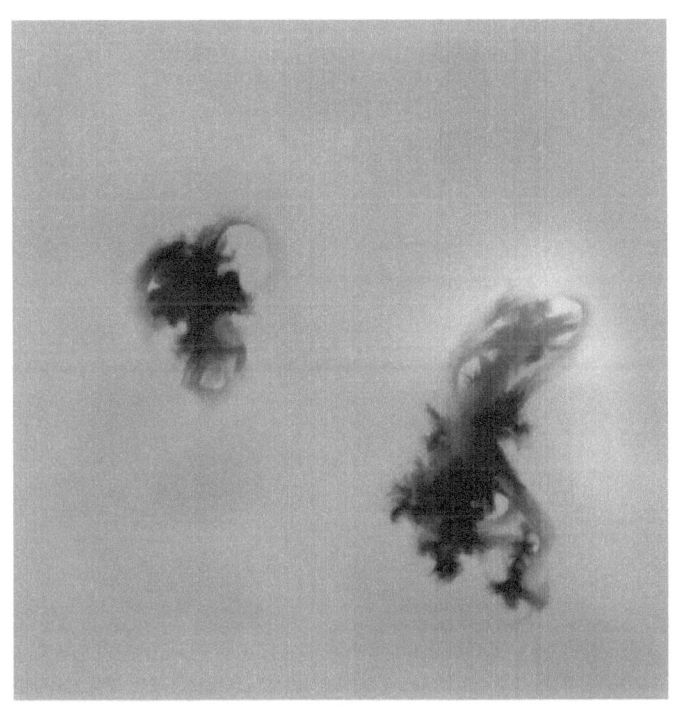

Contraptions

Venus Machine

The Day Angels Took Over the Machines

The day angels took over the machines someone
        whispered into the ear of a woman driving to
        work *we love you*
The day angels took over the machines children
        stopped laughing at man-made wonders and
        screamed into their lunchboxes into their
        mothers
The day angels took over the machines the wise and
        smiling ceased to smile and ceased being wise
It was as if one too many doors had been opened by
        benighted ingenuity cramped and greasy amid
        the ecstasy of meaningful lights a certain
        discreet savagery operating in the wings of
        voguey virtual sublimity
It was as if humankind had stumbled upon itself
        unrecognised undesired flexing unpredictable
        powers
It was as if humankind's unreasonable reason was
        suffering its first apoplexy of disbelief
The day angels took over the machines every speaker
        every headphone every telephone every TV
        every metallic throat pump-quivered
        we love you

The day angels took over the machines the world bled

    a single black tear the skies short-circuited in

    roseblush

The day angels took over the machines it was as if

    where are they running why aren't we running?

Suzuki's blaring eye and behind it mountainous

      blackness

Only a Matter of Time...

the violin's revenge:

a masterful blade

skating down

screaming

h u m a n

s k i n s

An Expert in His Field Examines an Antique Machine

What is it?

it has straight sides

and a glass bottom

the various coloured wires describe a sort of crown

or cage

the handle is made to fit the hand of a small child

or a trained monkey

the lubricating fluids

which one applies here here and here

can act as a mild irritant and should on no account

be imbibed or applied to the eyes

this broken spring is of the wrong type

the machine appears to function adequately

and as you can see this sudden forward motion

causes these dials to become excited

the raised discs

whose secondary purpose is to keep out the rain

or sunlight

would normally rotate at incredible speeds

and emit noises resembling those

of a rabid dog

or dramatic soprano

What is it?

these sharp angles are very interesting

and owe their existence to aesthetic rather than

practical considerations

if you look closely through this tiny aperture

you can see part of the nerve centre

so to speak

of the machine

this black lever or arm operates

the front or back of the machine

quite independently of the functions of the plastic

domes

What is it?

it's a counting machine propelled by steam and semen
which informs its owner of prayer-times and social
appointments facilitated by an ingenious system of
pulleys and microprocessors whose magnetic
properties enable the raised sections to dispense soft
drinks and eliminate political enemies though of course
not only politicians would own such machines whose
overall momentum is strictly monitored and controlled
by listening devices which owing to their cylindrical
shapes and capacity for metamorphosis at high

temperatures double up as miniature printing presses or alternatively as sterilisation units

Nude Falling Down a Staircase [Who pushed her?]

nude being pushed down a staircase

nude collapsing down a staircase

nude on a collapsing staircase

nude life ending on a staircase

nude ascending a staircase

nude going up in the world, plus staircase

nude negotiating a staircase

nude negotiating with a staircase

nude in heated discussion, plus staircase

nude on heat, plus staircase

nude on heat going down a staircase

nude on heat going down on her boyfriend, plus staircase

nude descending, minus staircase

nude descending no staircase

nude looking on horrified as the devil descends the staircase

nude making love to the devil under a staircase

nude in love on a staircase

nude in love with a staircase

nude inside a staircase

nude confirmed a nutcase

in case of nudity, descend stairs

Nude Falling Down a Staircase [You pushed her]

nude being pushed down a staircase

nude collapsing down a staircase

nude on a collapsing staircase

nude and staircase collapsing

nude falling down a staircase

nude falling to her death

nude life ending on a staircase

nude ascending a staircase

nude going up in the world, plus staircase

nude negotiating a staircase

nude negotiating with a staircase

nude in heated discussion, plus staircase

nude in the heat of the day on the staircase

nude on heat, plus staircase

nude on heat going down a staircase

nude on heat going down on her boyfriend, plus
staircase

nude on heat in the heat of the day going down on her
boyfriend on the staircase

nude going down

nude descending

nude descending, minus staircase

nude descending no staircase

nude falling through space

nude falling through eternity

nude falling to her damnation

nude devil falling down a staircase

nude looking on horrified as the devil descends the
staircase
nude looking on as the horny devil descends
nude making love to the devil under a staircase
nude under the sign of the devil
nude in love with the devil, plus staircase
nude in love on a staircase
nude in love with a staircase
nude in a staircase
nude trapped inside a staircase
nude confined within a staircase
nude confirmed a nutcase
nude's mental collapse on the staircase
nude collapsed on a staircase
nude collapsing down a staircase
nude being pushed down a staircase

murdered nude at the foot of the staircase
murdered muse at your feet

First Principles

I

She.

II

She lies.

III

She lies down.

IV

And down she lies.

V

He and she lie down.

VI

She lies and he is down.

VII

Earth is down; he and she lie.

VIII

She is the Earth. And he lies down.

IX

He and she are lying down in the earth.

X

He and she are lying, down in the red earth.

XI

When red, he and she are down in the earth, lying.

XII

The Earth: "And when is he lying?"
Down, she dreams in red.

XIII

And when she pushes dreams down, he is lying, red, in
the earth.

XIV

When he lies in her dreams the earth reddens and she
is pushed down.

XV

The Earth is a lie and when he, in dreams, pushes her
down, she reddens.

XVI

When her dream is lying in the earth he and she push
a red stone down.

XVII

Lying stoned and red, she dreams he pushes her down.
When is a coffin in the earth?

XVIII

He lies dreaming in a red coffin. She pushes the stony
earth. And when her hair is down...

René & Renée

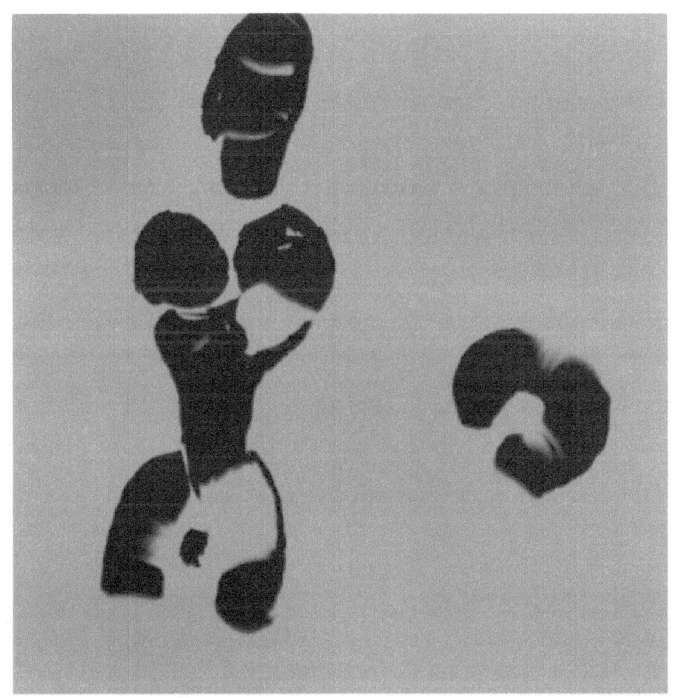

Prototype

A Life Begins

René was born with a scream in the city of sighs.

His mother was a gloop of love and syrup, his father a ruined statue. They occupied their separate zones of existence and René occupied his. They seldom saw each other, save sometimes on the landing or outside on the street. When they did meet they usually failed to recognise each other. Seeing her son, René's mother would burst into tears and fall in love with the little darling, dandling him in her massive formless hands, wondering who he was, wondering if her lost son was anything like him. At such times, René felt lifeless. He hung limply in the maternal folds.

When René was nine his father mistook him for a burglar and shot his face off with the shotgun he had bought on holiday. After the mishap René visited Dr Goitre, who gave him several new faces, one for each day of the week. So René was able to change who he was whenever he wanted.

On the morning of his thirtieth birthday, having put on his favourite face, René went out into the world and met the beautiful Renée for the first time. Their meeting was brief but full of promise. Since then, René has searched the continents and oceans and stars for the miraculous woman who made him feel love. But the land and sea and exploding universe keep their secrets under jealous guard, and to date poor René has had no joy.

He is to be seen, every day, walking along the same deserted beach, the sun glaring in his eyes, his phantom footprints forever being erased by the terrible silent sea.

Birth

At noon the sun broke in two and spilt its yoke over the deserted city. The yoke fell into a square surrounded by ruined facades, where presently a shape struggled to rise out of the sticky goo. At first spherical, it then sprouted two arms and two legs. As it stood up, the searing yellow slid down its body and collected in a pool at its feet. It was Renée, the first woman. She looked exactly as you imagine her.

She trod unsteadily away from the sun's last light (now nothing more than a large puddle) and smiled as she beheld the avenues and alleyways luxuriating in darkness and extending away into infinity.

The world was cool and black. Renée felt quite at home. She glanced up at the stars and read there an obscure destiny.

Then she lost herself in the lightless city.

Night Wrestling

Every night his bed became the arena in which René wrestled with his dreams. He pounded at shapeless things, he convulsed under the pall of the sheets, he strained to push away the velvet tentacles sliding over his body. Very often a dream would insinuate its vapours into his lungs, making him cough and retch, or it would cover his feverish body with thousands of insects, scratching and biting. His neighbours got used to the nightly thuds and screams, so much so that after a while they ceased to be conscious of the noise, and their murmuring dreams of wheat and twilight flowed uninterrupted.

Next time you are kept awake by toothache or insomnia or mosquitoes, pity poor René, who struggles against dreams night after night, on a sweat-soaked battlefield.

Jealousy

René came home one day in a fit of jealousy. He slammed the front door behind him and kicked the cat as it lay sleeping on the carpet in the hallway. The frightened creature hissed venomously and fled upstairs.

Renée came out of the living room and asked René what was the matter? He told her she was a slut and that he had put up with it for long enough. He grabbed her raven hair and pulled it savagely, telling her she must confess her adulteries.

When Renée refused to confess René held her forehead in his trembling left hand, and with the right hand slowly drew from his wife's ear one of the men he suspected of having slept with her. The man emerged thin and brittle, from having been in Renée's mind for so long. René stood him on the carpet and laughed at this miserable, insubstantial Lothario. Then he kicked him in the balls, making him shatter like glass.

Gripping Renée by the forehead again, René pulled another brittle stickman from her ear, and again he set him on the carpet, laughed derisively and destroyed him with a kick to the crotch.

René went on like this for some time, pulling men from his wife's ear and sending their fragments flying over the hallway, until they were knee-deep in pieces of libertine. Whenever René moved his feet they crunched and crackled. Looking inside Renée's ear, he realised there were still many more men inhabiting his wife's mind. He cleared a space on the carpet and sat down, cross-legged and dispirited.

Renée laughed at him; he looked so silly, like a sulking brat! She waded over to her husband, kissed his forehead and said she was going to get a dustpan and brush.

From the top of the stairs, the injured cat looked down on René like the devil gloating at the damned.

Metamorphosis

In the most popular version of the myth, Renée exploded into womanhood with the suddenness and violence of a bomb going off. It all happened in the space of a few seconds. Breasts erupted from the hitherto featureless surface of her chest; a mesh of little hairs covered her pudenda like a protective hand; sighs and desires made her breathing urgent and laboured. Most disturbingly she bled profusely, her menses scorching down her legs, flooding the pavements of the ruined city, drowning the little girls who lay sleeping in their beds. Wracked by fever and convulsions, Renée fled the city and threw herself at the first man she met, a minstrel from across the sea. She covered him, she tore kisses from his mouth, she smothered him, she sucked the life from him. And then she left him, desiccated and shrunken, on the hot smooth sands.

In a variant of this version of events, Renée is said to have *willed herself* into her state of paroxysmal womanhood. People who subscribe to this account have no pity for her, and tend to regard her as a sorceress.

A more sympathetic version of the myth has it that Renée's metamorphosis from little girl to sexual woman was the result of some insult she had unwittingly made to one of the gods (Jehovah is usually named as the creature of hurt pride), and the transformation itself lasted several excruciating hours. So weak and drained of blood was she by the end of the ordeal, she survived thanks only to the benevolence of a passing clown, who cut open his jugular vein and let her drink until she was fully restored to health, if not to her former self. What happened to the clown after this act of self-sacrifice is unknown.

There is a fourth school of thought on the metamorphosis of Renée, which maintains that she simply *grew up* in the same way as all girls the world over. However, this theory is too mundane to be treated seriously by anyone of intelligence or imagination.

Escape

René often felt the need to get away from himself. He felt suffocated by who he was, tied down to his own body and mind. So he would stand up suddenly on the train, hoping to leave himself behind on the seat, a shrivelled husk. Or he would run along the tree-lined avenues, kicking through dead leaves, his belly full of panic, desperate to tear away from himself, imagining himself as another brown leaf that might fall at any moment.

Of course, nothing ever happened. His body, his mind, his fears, desires, guts, hair, confusions, flesh, clung together, inseparable.

René would always be heavy with who he was, a stone sinking perpetually in a black lake.

Making Babies

René and Renée were sitting up in bed one night, reading. René was reading a collection of pornographic murder stories in which the detective, Goon, always turned out to be the killer. Renée, meanwhile, was reading her palm. She sighed and put her hand down and said to her husband, "Why don't we have children?"

Poor René did not know if this was a suggestion or another example of his wife's ignorance regarding biological processes. What should he say? He put down his book (at the best bit: Goon was just about to garrotte his chief suspect) and turned to his wife, wondering how on earth he could begin to explain the whole nasty business of conception, gestation and birth. She said, "Why don't we have children? Just one or two would be fine, for now." Ah! so it was a suggestion! René turned down the corner of page 97 of *Goon's Casebook* (unable to resist reading, as he did so, a fragment of a sentence near the top of the page, which ran, with characteristic verve: "... and notwithstanding the moral weight of professional obligation devolving to him in these circumstances, Goon, after expatiating on the matter with some feeling, drew to a conclusion to him as distasteful as it was ineluctable, and began preparations for the execution of an act which would, conducted with dignity and sensitivity, perhaps permit him to consider afresh ..."), yes René actually put the beloved book on his bedside cabinet without finishing the story, and then stroked his wife's cheek with the back of his hand.

"Let's make babies," he said.

So they did.

An hour or two after their lovemaking, Renée felt about ready to give birth. Her belly was big and round and covered with red stretch marks. She could feel something squirming inside her, feeling for a way out. So she woke René up from his dream (in which he was Goon, drawing up a list of suspects and devising interrogation techniques) and said, "I'm about to give birth. Do something!"

René panicked. His wife's gestation period was a good few hours shorter than he had expected. He ran out into the street, wailing.

Renée was on her own. She closed her eyes and held her breath, until, with an appalling popping sound, she felt one then two then three then four then five then *six* lithe creatures heave out of her womb. She opened her eyes. One of her babies was just a leg, but a very nice leg (and extraordinarily well developed! thought Renée), and it was hopping happily about the room.

Another was made up of odds and ends of offal, and but for the child's horrid stench he (or she?) was quite delightful. A third was a big head, black and wrinkled, which clung to the undersheet by its teeth. The others were, it has to be said, something of a disappointment to their mother. One was a saucepan, another was an electric kettle, and the last was a roll of lavatory paper. Renée wept as she looked at them; they were so domestic, so banal! They would never be great poets or magicians or space explorers! She wept and wept, and her tears flowed out of the window and cascaded to the street below.

Ten years later René returned home. He had had a wonderful decade, travelling, eating soup, reading the latest Goon sagas. As he walked into the flat he smiled at his wife, who was sitting on the sofa, reading her palm.

"How's things?" said René.

"Not bad," replied Renée, and she explained to him all that had happened in his absence: her upbringing of the children, their schooling, their departure for foreign climes, their return, their marriages and homosexual relationships, their illnesses, their deaths. They had had a good life, she said, although she hinted that three of them had not made the most of their opportunities.

René was satisfied. Clearly the baby project had been a success, more or less. He sat next to his beloved wife and said, "I love you."

Then they went to bed. The moon and the stars shone with extra vigour that night, so glad were they to see husband and wife reunited. Those clouds that wandered too close to the moon were lit up with its white heat.

René and Renée lay in the marital bed, in a still embrace.

"Let's make more babies," said René. And his wife, of course, agreed.

The Bad Leg

René woke up one beautiful July morning to find something was wrong. As he moved to get out of bed he felt a shooting pain in his left leg. He had never felt such a pain before. He got out of bed and walked around the bedroom, testing the leg, making sure it bent at the knee and supported him. It was working fine, but the pain was a torment, a burning of the marrow.

René didn't trust doctors. He remembered when his father had gone to hospital for a heart operation and came back with no ears. It was months before René could look at him without laughing. There was no way René was going to risk ending up like that, an object of ridicule to be smirked at in the street. However, the pain in his left leg was making him cry. It wouldn't hurt just to consult a doctor. He needn't consent to surgery or pills. Knowing what was causing the pain might be enough to help him cope with it.

***

René opened the door and stepped into a small room. At one end there was a desk with a computer and a couple of chairs. There was a door, slightly ajar, leading into another, even smaller room. René glanced into the other room and saw a high bed with white sheets and a large wall chart made up of mystifying symbols and diagrams.

There was a man sitting behind the desk, caressing the computer keyboard. He was bald and extremely short, and his nose was shaped like a parsnip. Without looking up at René he told him in a surprisingly deep voice to take a seat. One of the little hands flickered in the direction of a chair. René did as he was told, stretching out his left leg (still hurting), to give the man a clue as to why he was there.

The bald man abruptly stopped touching the computer keys and swivelled his head so that his squinting eyes came to rest on René's afflicted leg. He asked René what seemed to be the matter with him. René explained about the pain and, standing up and walking around the room, showed the little man that he was quite capable of using his leg as normal. What could it mean?

The man had answers up his sleeve, no doubt, to all such questions. What could it mean, indeed? He told René to remove his trousers and walk about. He squeezed the muscles on the afflicted leg. He asked questions about René's work, about his leisure activities, about his love life. He rummaged in an enormous gladstone bag which sat on the floor like a fat toad, and brought out some shiny black instruments, with which he prodded, scratched and rubbed various parts of René's body, not just the leg.

Finally, as René stood, trouserless, in the centre of the room, the bald man performed a sort of dance around him, making little exclamations in some alien tongue. Then he told him to put his trousers back on and sit down.

***

Three months later René was on a trolley, being wheeled through antiseptic corridors towards the operating theatre in which the bad leg would be removed forever. It was the right thing to do. The man with the parsnip-shaped nose had been most insistent that the pain would never disappear otherwise. To prove it, he had prescribed various potent pain-killers, none of which had stopped the shooting, burning sensation. René had hardly slept since the trouble began. Now he thought with relish of his revenge on the bad leg. He would soon show it who was boss.

***

It was a mild November morning and René was waking up from a dreamless slumber. He felt great. He sat up in bed and looked across the room at his favourite ornament, a huge glass case filled with formaldehyde and containing his malevolent left leg. He laughed out loud and pointed at the estranged limb, saying, "Who's laughing now?" The leg was sickly and pale and slightly shrivelled. René was exultant.

He lay back for a moment, and as he did so he suffered a most disagreeable sensation. It felt for a second as if the bad leg was still attached to him. He experienced a stabbing pain coming from the empty space where his leg used to be. In a fright, he shoved the duvet away, to reassure himself that the leg really was gone. Sure enough, his right leg had no companion. René looked back up at the bad leg in the glass case. Still there. By now the pain had gone. René sighed and smiled. It was nothing. Everything was fine.

***

A week later René visited the bald little man with the parsnip-shaped nose again. He parked his wheelchair in front of the desk. The space where his left leg used to be burned like acid. He had been in constant agony for three days, and was at his wits' end.

The strange man helped René to get his trousers off and examined the space where the bad leg used to be, squinting intently at the nothingness. He placed a quivering hand over where the limb would have been and moved it back and forth, thoughtfully. René fancied that from somewhere in the distance, almost drowned out by the waves of pain, he could make out the sensation of his nonexistent leg being stroked. The man fished around in his baleful gladstone bag and brought out a pair of binoculars, and continued his examination of the non-leg with their aid, as if searching for something millions of miles away. Then he said, "Aha!" and nodded, and down went the binoculars.

René asked for an explanation. The bald man wore an inexplicable smile as he told René that, although his leg was technically and from a scientific point of view quite dead, it had continued to live in some distant dimension and hence existed in our world as a phantom. As far as Nature is concerned phantoms aren't real, so you can't get rid of them, he enthused. René didn't understand a word of what was being said to him. Either his leg was there or it wasn't. He asked the man what he could do to stop the pain, which was bringing tears to his eyes again. The man shrugged and said, with the smug smile that René now wanted to punch very hard, that there was nothing anyone could do about it. René's would be a life of irremediable pain. No pills or alternative treatments or psychotherapy would ever make the slightest difference.

He asked if René wouldn't mind closing the door behind him on his way out.

***

Back home, René sat in front of his preserved leg. It looked somehow different now from the way it used to be. It no longer appeared pale or shrivelled. In fact, it was the picture of health, pink and robust. The pain in René's phantom leg increased.

René noticed his reflection in the tall mirror to his right. He was haggard and his skin had taken on the shiny texture of plastic. His eyes were hollow and glassy. It was like looking at a stranger or at a gruesome model in a spooky fairground ride. Sleeplessness and anxiety were draining him of his life. In an absurd moment he pictured the preserved leg smashing out of its glass case, splattering him with formaldehyde as it leapt onto his chest. The toenails had become talons, which gripped him by the neck, and a little mouth with two sharp fangs appeared in the sole and feasted on his throat. He could feel the lifeblood being sucked out of him.

René decided that the only solution was to get rid of the preserved leg.

***

That evening saw a thin, broken figure with one leg and a bulging bin liner tucked under his arm hobbling on crutches towards the lake by the petrified forest. The moonlight showed him the way along a dusty path, towards the deserted beach. The water lapped the stones in slow motion, back and forth, back and forth.

René opened the bin liner to get one last look at his amputated limb. It was silvery and weird in the moonlight. Having put some large stones in with the leg (itself a tricky feat for a man so disadvantaged), he tied the top of the bin liner and chucked it into the lake, which accepted the gift with a gentle splash. Then he went home.

As everybody knows, if you throw an amputated limb into a lake sooner or later it will decompose, until all that is left of it is bone. That's how Nature works. René's left leg was no exception, and it rotted swiftly in its leaky rubber coffin.

Unfortunately, the phantom leg was here to stay. If only René had trusted his doctor's prognosis! The triumph of watching the bin liner sink into the lake allowed René a brief respite from his pain, but by the time he was back home the mischievous phantom was up to its old tricks. Limping through the front door, René shook with agony. The crutches fell away from him and he fell flat onto his face. Lying there, his arms sprawled, he felt his phantom leg burn. Incredulity gave way to despair. He had no more strength. He was a spent man. He sobbed into the carpet made bloody by his broken nose.

So the bad leg had the last laugh.

On Waking

Renée opened her eyes to find an alien world. She was in a room she did not recognise, swimming in colours and forms. The scents of the new world, pouring from the mouths of eyeless creatures with green necks, made her giddy, and the strange music of the space beyond the walls of the room enchanted and terrified her. She did not know where she was or who she was or why she was. Every part of her trembled to know.

She tried to remember. Impressions of her life sped through her mind. She was an airhostess. No, she was a boxer, bloody and undefeated. No, she was a little girl lost in her sister's wendy-house. She was a rhinoceros. She was a cloud. Each idea was as valid as the last, and all were equally uncertain.

Exactly half a second after opening her eyes, she remembered that she was Renée. Two seconds after that, she was convinced of the rightness of this identity. The room was no longer unfamiliar; it settled into recognition. She recognised the flowers in the vase on the chest-of-drawers and the police sirens outside on the street. Everything was as it should be.

Renée sat up in bed and remembered René, that part of her life not present in the room. She looked at the photo of him she kept on her bedside cabinet. He smiled sadly at her. She was overcome with the longing to be with him, and then she remembered that she would be with him, that evening, when they met for dinner.

Renée was glad of the certainties she had attained within ten seconds of waking. She got out of bed and walked automatically towards the door. Opening it, she looked back at the impression left by her body on the ruffled undersheet and felt a flush of fearful delight at the prospect of tomorrow's waking confusion.

Coming of Age

On the evening of his last day of childhood René wept like a baby. All of the certainties he had clung to, all the simple securities would be gone by tomorrow, and he would be expected to behave like an adult and know all about the world. He would have to say goodbye to his toys and teddy-bears and picture books, and amuse himself instead with women, drugs and jazz music. He sobbed as he considered the comforts that would be snatched from him in a matter of hours. No more would his parents shelter, feed and clothe him. They had packed his suitcase and gone to bed early, ready to rise at dawn tomorrow to conduct the ceremonial expulsion of their son, a ritual that would be witnessed and enjoyed by the whole neighbourhood. As René cried he promised himself that no matter what happened to him he would never forsake his childhood, he would always carry an imaginary teddy-bear with him, and his progress through the world of adulthood would amount to a carefully managed fraud, a pretence at maturity. In his most apparently adult behaviour, slouching drunkenly in bars whilst cheap women picked his pockets, he would still be a child, inward looking and disdainful of the fallen world into which he had been thrust against his will.

The moon shone through the grimy window and cast a mocking light on René's distress. He looked up at that ridiculous muse of unimaginative poets, that cold piece of space rock, and some of his sorrow became anger as he considered what his mother had told him earlier that evening, that the moon turned girls into women by exerting its gravitational pull on their chests, inflating and distorting them into such monstrous excrescences that they go mad with anxiety and cease to be little girls any more. His mother had also told him, with a solemn nodding of her head, that it was thanks to the metamorphosis of girls into women that little boys had to grow up too. He had questioned how this worked, but her reply had been simply, "Tomorrow you will understand!" Poor, uncomprehending René! How he hated the moon for its indirect and baleful influence on his life!

There was also the horrible possibility that tomorrow's entry into the adult world might have some physical consequences for René. He remembered being told by one of his classmates that when boys turn into men fur appears all over their torsos, and their penises acquire independent will, growing and shrinking when they please, often against the wishes of their owners. The same classmate also dropped dark hints about a sticky substance released by these capricious penises, a milky discharge symptomatic of the malaise of adulthood. René was horrified to learn that some women collected this foul liquid and stored it in their stomachs, where it fed millions of maggots that would one day burst out of their hosts, killing them in the process, and roam the earth as monsters. What if all this were true? How would he cope with a rebellious penis and a world inhabited by monsters? He looked again at the moon and intoned against it a curse he had learned from the witch next door, over and over until exhaustion claimed him and he slept.

René's dreams that night were even more distressing than usual. In one he found himself trapped in the body of a bear and every time he tried to cry for help his throat emitted an appalling roar. In another he was drowning in a swamp. He had dreams of violence and dreams of bereavement. Matricide and patricide featured as recurring motifs. He found himself successively strangling, stabbing, poisoning, shooting, garrotting, suffocating and drowning his parents. He looked impassively at their faces, which were dehumanised by their suffering. He felt at once thrilled, nauseous and numb. In the strangest dream he would have that night he sprouted breasts, heavy and plump, which he caressed with mad joy until they burst, releasing into the air clouds of spores like talcum powder. In all of these dreams René was simultaneously participant and voyeur, collaborator and conniver, protagonist and victim, aggressor and helpless onlooker. So when dawn arrived and he was awoken by the rough hand of his father he was relieved to be leaving behind the confusions of sleep.

His relief was short-lived. Looking up at the old man, he remembered what today was. "Get up, son. It's time," said his father, with a curiously melancholy look in his eyes that belied the oafish grin he always wore for special occasions. René sat up in bed. Outside, in the street, people were chattering excitedly. He recognised the pompous voice of Mr Mort the Circus Master and the laughter of Renée, his next-door neighbour's daughter. Everyone was waiting for the grand expulsion. How they loved a good drama! A golden dawn suffused the room with its expectant light.

René's father stood and stared and grinned.

Monsters

René's early adulthood was characterised by the appearance, all around him, of monsters. They were legion. Sitting in stations, walking around bookshops, queuing for cinema tickets, eating soup, laughing and conversing, driving buses, these monsters were everywhere. They didn't even have the decency to look like people. Many were crazy mishmashes of familiar animals, with unblinking shark eyes and frisky feline tails, or bizarre arrangements of tusks and teeth emerging from rainbow plumage. Others were made of a cracked, brittle substance which made their movements small and jerky. Others still seeped about as thick liquids, black and stinking. All of these creatures got on very nicely with the human race; indeed, human beings had long ago lost the power to distinguish between man and monster, so society ticked over and all lived harmoniously.

René was not frightened of the monsters (how could he be, when his nightmares were far uglier?), but he found their preponderance disquieting, as if their constant presence was a sign of bad things to come.

On the morning of his thirtieth birthday René was swallowed whole by a monster which had fallen from the skies with a tremendous explosion and had then eaten its way through most of the burning city. The creature's name was Renée. It was identical to René himself in every way, except that it was twenty times his size and had a gaping vagina for a mouth. It wasn't a bad monster, just painfully hungry. All it could do was eat.

As René swam in the digestive juices of his monstrous double he ruminated that life in this stomach wasn't so bad; after all, he was warm and safe, and wouldn't have to worry about having to do anything ever again. He could just stretch out and share his host's gargantuan meals and sleep whenever he wanted.

His only fear now was being shat out of Renée's fearsome anus. He didn't want to experience the agony of birth into the cold, cold world for a second time. You could say that this thought prevented him from becoming too complacent in his new luxury. Whenever he supped on the latest mangled morsels to come pumping down Renée's gullet, he said a word of thanks to God for looking after him. Similarly, he learned to be grateful for the little death of sleep, which nowadays was dreamless and lovely. No more wrestling with images! Unable to see anything in the profound blackness of Renée during his waking hours, he found that his sleep too was undisturbed by pictures. He was free.

Romance

René was wracked with pain. His stomach was in revolt and he had a high temperature. Lying in his sick bed he sweated and stewed like a pig on a spit.

Several times during his fever he called out for Renée, but she was elsewhere, in another world altogether. He knew this, but he called anyway, straining his throat and burning lungs to cough out her name.

Later on, in the cool of evening, bathed in shadows, he was able to sit up in bed. He was parched. He lifted a glass of water from the little table at his bedside and, closing his eyes, let it eel down his throat. This was a mistake. His stomach objected to the cold water and heaved vengefully. René had no time to move; a shower of watery puke exploded from his nose and mouth.

René looked at the mess on the duvet and was immediately transported with joy. By some incredible coincidence, his vomit had arranged itself in such a way as to suggest the face of his beloved, the elusive Renée. There were her sparkling eyes, and look! there was her smile. He could imagine nothing more beautiful than that smile.

René gazed and gazed at the marvellous portrait until the envious shadows of night had effaced it completely.

Impressions from a Birth

Bawling eelslippery bloody child.

Maternal sobs.

Just as labour begins a cockroach falls from the ceiling and lands on her stomach. This is such a filthy hospital! Maternal and paternal eyes converge on the insect. They read it like an omen.

Little baby René won't open his eyes. He can't accept this cold world of sharp noises! His father, the colonel, picks him up and holds him close to his face. René can sense that he is being examined. He opens one eye and sees his father's vast red features, then immediately closes it and turns his head away. Never again will he look at the world!

As the first contractions begin, the cockroach falling.

The baby impatient to leave its den.

The colonel standing with his hands behind his back, watching impassively as his wife heaves out something raw and bawling.

Renée's tears of terror of regret of joy of delirium of discomfort of impatience of mirth of despair of indifference. Her baby fists beating the air.

The squirm and shriek of her mother's body.

René screws up his face, regretting his haste. It is an end to warmth and darkness.

The cockroach scuttling from a mound of round flesh to the starched undersheet, then falling to the floor.

Renée's father picks her up in his claws and regards her with a suspicious and bloodshot eye. She contorts under his scrutiny.

The cockroach falling.

Under his unblinking gaze, her legs open, her panting and sobbing, the spasms.

A beautiful baby!

The colonel holds the baby upside-down by the ankles and inspects its genitals. He can't be sure of what he's looking at. The child is nothing but flesh and noise.

Renée is enraptured at having escaped the prison of her mother's womb. When they cut the umbilical cord she nearly faints with pleasure.

As the climax approaches a cockroach falls from the ceiling and lands on her stomach. This is such a filthy hotel! Eyes converge on the insect. She isn't put off, though, and she can feel the moment arriving.

The colonel standing with his hands over his eyes, as his wife heaves out something raw and bawling.

René decides to turn on the waterworks, knowing that this will secure a place in his parents' affections. His cries are also a fanfare for his momentous birth.

The cockroach falls from the ceiling, while below Renée's mother screws up her face and clenches her fists.

The maternal body: bloody, open, raw.

The cockroach, landing on her belly at the moment of the decisive spasm, is taken to be an omen that this child will not have an easy life.

She sobs. The hotel light flickers.

The colonel looks on, impassive.

The Small Hours

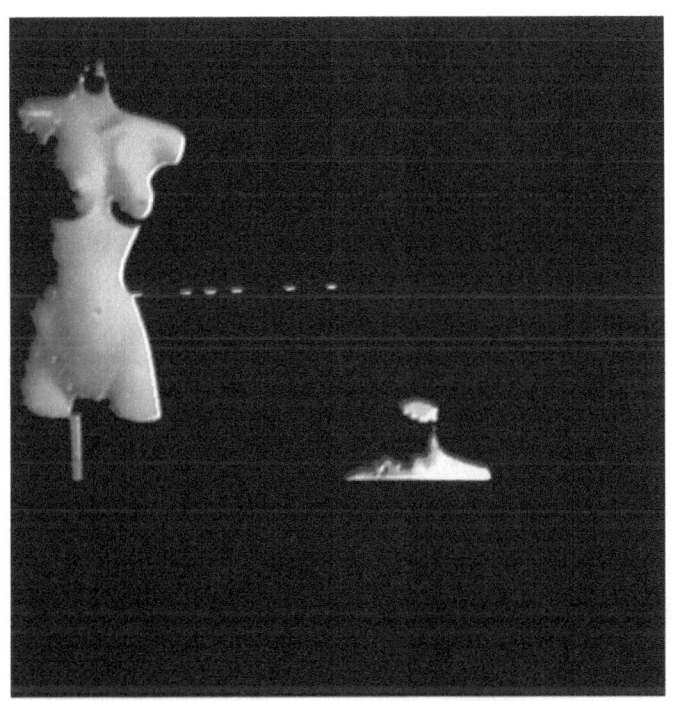

A Trick of the Light

Entrance

No sleep now for three nights. Grey dawns, birdsong, a shaky hand holding a coffee mug. Lights turning on and off all over the world. He catches his wasted reflection in the mirror over the fireplace.

Sitting at his desk, he looks once more at the photographic evidence he has collected. Pictures taken from a slight distance, cluttered with irrelevance: people, cars, houses, pigeons, genteel suburban trees. But somewhere in the midst of every one of them is a glimpse of the murder victim. In many she is walking hurriedly, eyes down, shoulders slightly hunched, dark hair obscuring her face. In some he has managed to catch her in a brief moment of stillness, locking her front door or waiting to cross the road. His favourite is the one of her sitting on the green that she used to walk through every day on her way to the newsagent's; in this one she is cross-legged on an old rug, a bottle of water by her bare feet, reading some trashy thriller with a picture of a child's doll on the cover. The doll is twisted and broken, a battered corpse. A strange little smile plays on her lips.

He lifts this last photo to the light and traces her outline with a finger.

No sleep now for three nights. Three nights since she was found murdered in her own home, in her own bed, in a room at the top of the house. Since then, a media explosion, cameras and reporters on the high street, at neighbours' doors, on the green where she had sat, that beautiful day in August. In death her celebrity has multiplied. Once a respected actress in TV crime dramas, she is now an icon. The mystery of the demise of this beautiful young woman obsesses the nation.

Seventeen hours later he is sitting on a street bench, opposite her house. It is dark and no one is around. Not even a policeman stationed outside the crime scene. It starts to rain. The last grisly news update was delivered from this spot by a scrawny suit with slicked-back, thinning hair, five hours ago. Police tape forms a criss-cross over the front door of the house. The forensic people won't be back until the morning. He checks his pockets for the camera, note-book, pen, torch and knife, then he stands up and crosses the road.

He needs to see everything for himself, every detail. Some sense has to be made of this. He cuts the police tape and stands before the front door. The buzzing in his ears is back. Dots and flashes, an untuned TV gauze between him and the external world. For now the world is simply that door. Nothing else exists. He feels sick, faint. He squats and an automatic hand lifts the large flowerpot that the police, amazingly, have not examined. Underneath is her spare key.

No choice but to go inside. Exhausted, nervous, light-headed, brimming with dark dreams, he inserts the key. He knows that from this moment he is lost.

Vertigo

Pictorial I

Eyes wide. Head up. Snap snap snap. Steady hands pull dark hair away from her face. And smile. The shutter's swift mechanism. She climbs two more stairs, turns to face him, one hand on the handrail. That's beautiful. The hallway strobes. Flash flash flash. Lightning and desire. She sits on a stair, pulls her skirt up a little. Legs together, side on. He moves in. Lips part, a tongue pokes between white teeth. The rest of the world has gone to sleep. Snap snap. Stand up again. Her back to the camera, looking over her right shoulder. Locks of dark hair fall forward, obliterating her face. The shutter's maniacal hunger for her. Snap snap snap snap snap. Chin held defiantly, eyes full of callous pride. The flickering hallway. That's lovely. Images explode in his shuttered mind. Right, let's try something on the first floor landing.

Take Five

Alessandra Lucenti, considered by many to be the world's most beautiful film star, sits before the mirror in her dressing room. She wears a light gown and her dark hair is pinned up. Her chin rests on her hands as she gazes impassively into the reflection of her famously seductive eyes.

"Now remember that Carla has no idea that this man is going to kill her later in the movie. As far as she's concerned, he's just a regular guy. So you're not putting up too many defences, okay?"

Alessandra Lucenti nods somewhat impatiently in the direction of the voice, then turns again to the tall man whose hands have repositioned themselves, one in the small of her back, one grazing her neck. The voice again: "And action!" As Carla White, Alessandra Lucenti allows the imposing figure to caress her freely. She tilts her head back and grips his waist. Her eyes close as he pulls her towards him, and then he is kissing her neck. The man's scent is bitter, oppressive, suffocating. She stumbles backwards.

"Now what is it? That was looking good! Please, just let the scene unfold. Don't keep putting the brakes on."

She closes her eyes again. The man moves in on her and suddenly his lips are on hers. He grabs the back of her head with both hands and delivers his line, in a histrionic, breathless whisper. Alessandra Lucenti nearly laughs in his face, but Carla White is learning to do as the director says and automatically, out of nowhere, comes her line, her answer to his. The words are meaningless, mere decoration. More lines follow, a vacuous dialogue in which nothing is said that hasn't already been communicated by the lovers' embrace and the man's aggressive affection.

Alessandra Lucenti has fallen asleep.

Staring into her own eyes, reflected in the depths, drunk with her own beauty.

She cannot breathe, she begins to panic. Arms thrash, her back arches. She can feel his presence towering over her, an iron shadow. Opening her eyes, all she can see is a dark shimmering. Her cry emerges muffled and weak. The man shifts his position and she feels herself falling away from him, into the darkness.

"That's great," says the director, dragging on a cigarette, "only next time, could we stick to the script?"

Masque Ball 3

They can see Lexa Lux cavorting in the rainbow reflections of the ballroom mirrors. Cameras try to fix her fleeting smile. A corset bulging with wank thrills, teeth flashing like knives. A bird mask covers her upper face, red feathers bleed into the smoky air. Legs blur in a haze of quickstep stocking. Round and round her go the other dancers, princes and queens, masters and mistresses, glamorous nightmares. The string quartet hastens to a frenzy as they spin and stamp.

Lexa has to find her prey. He is on the other side of the ballroom, seated by the ornate fireplace, hidden behind the skirts of two girls in golden masks. Lexa catches a glimpse of him in a mirror and moves in. Violin strings are scratched to breaking point. Dancers part, spilling out of her way. Lexa swoops down on him as the gold-masked girls step to one side. Cameras follow like vultures, alighting in a semi-circle around the scene now being enacted by the bird queen and the seated man. She feasts on him, her black beak prodding his naked belly.

Reflections multiply, the lighting changes, clothes fall off bronze bodies, black bodies, I shake my head and sink down, crying, to the floor.

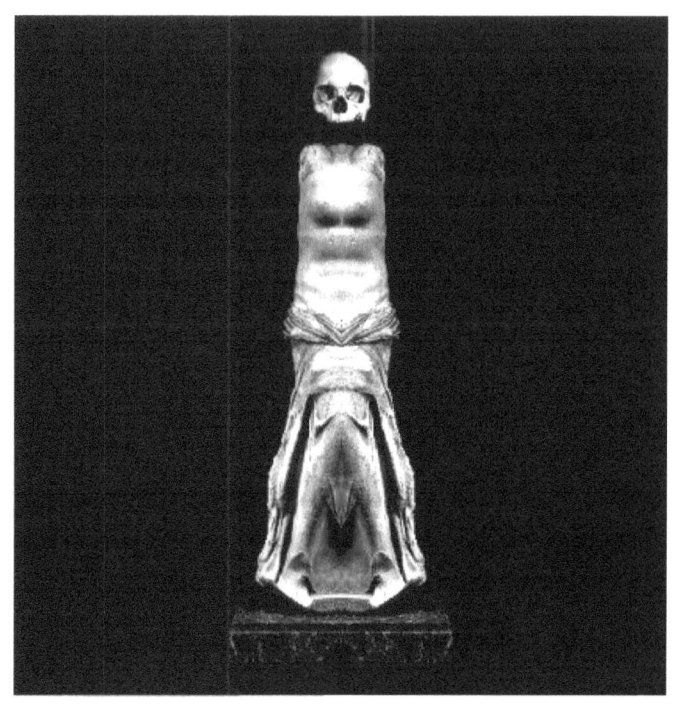

Venus, la mort

Eat

Closing his eyes, pressing his fingers to his eyelids, he pictures her as an Arcimboldo assemblage of fruits. Peach cheeks, strawberry lips, sliced kiwi eyes. Her hair is a froth of blackberries. He can imagine her only from the neck up, a portrait in half-profile. The rest of her does not exist or cannot be conceived.

The fluorescent tube stutters, pulses. A world of undertakings and abortive plans. He struggles to remember their first and only meeting, the where and when, but she floats singular and contextless over the landscape of his life. His pen scratches dry paper, doodling, searching for something concrete in disconnected memories. Swirls and spirals spin randomly on the page. He had intended to write, but that's impossible. He had hoped to reconstruct her through an objective account, free of tiresome literary clutter, bringing her into focus through precise description; but there is nothing to describe. He sees her through a prism. Her iridescence is evasive, dispiriting; her obliviousness to him, a mockery.

Rain patters against the window, and beyond that is darkness. He smirks at the triteness of pathetic fallacy. The fluorescent tube beats a quiet tattoo, reminding him of a dream sequence in a third-rate film. He closes his eyes again and sees a bowl of rotting fruit.

Pictorial II

Now stop there but don't turn around. One foot on the floor of the landing, the other on the top stair. Painted red nails on the handrail, the curve of buttock cheeks. Flash flash flash flash. Great, now turn your head to your right and look down at me. Light bursting, whitening her to a ghost. A smile: teeth and eyes. He climbs a few more steps. She turns to face him. The camera, up close, takes her in fragments: skirt hitched, knees together; top strap falling off a shoulder; a look of playful irony. The hallway appears, disappears with each flash. Another step up. You are looking so hot. She stands on the landing, hands on hips. Snap snap. Just pull your top up a little, show us your piercing. A lock of black hair falling over her face. Perfumed poses, bittersweet as love. Those eyes that see through everything, through him. A tiny ball of steel in a bellybutton. Flash flash flash. He wants to document every inch. One more like that; I'm just gonna come in closer. This is easy for her. The hallway fills with her laughter and she wiggles her impossible body. The camera snaps at her flesh, greedily inhales her.

Night

He wakes up with the shivers, thinking of her. A breeze enters through the open sash window, the curtain moves with the ghost of her presence. It is still dark.

He heaves himself upright, limbs stiff and cold. The night is a desert. His parched senses drink in the darkness, draw it in, in the hope that she might have left some trace in the air: her scent, the black murmur of her voice, the white suppleness of her back. Nothing.

Sometimes he feels like a man drowning, suffocated by the idea of her. Or someone falling in slow motion down the innumerable steps of a spiral staircase, his descent that of a lost soul who does not even have the consolation of Hell to look forward to. He knows that he can never reach the bottom, that his fall will be eternal.

She is poisonous. She whispers sweet venom while he dreams. Intangible as love, she coils around him, gripping his torso, a hissing phantom.

He gets out of bed and walks to the window. Drawing back the curtain, he looks out onto the square and the faint drizzle blurring under streetlights. On the other side of the square there is a house that is the exact mirror image of his own. Despite the poor light, he can just discern a shape, a suggestion of movement in an open window on the first floor. It is a man, leaning out, head hung, hands clasped.

He prays for an end to this.

The Rules of the Game

Scene 17

"And action!"

Two figures silhouetted against the glowing backdrop of the bedroom. As Carla White, Alessandra Lucenti breaks down, sobbing, falling to the floor. Hands over face, shaking. The actor who plays her husband stands by, helpless, not knowing what comes next.

Or he has a stocking over his head and a gun in his hand. He will shoot her and she will clutch at him, sobbing (as if she knows that it is her own husband who has disguised himself and attacked her), sobbing, bleeding, limping to the bed when he pushes her away in alarm and disgust, collapsing, bleeding profusely, trying to say his name but unable, calling out to him or condemning him, impossible to tell, a white hand, a thin white hand thrust towards him, beseeching or accusatory, it could be either, the tears and tears, an outpouring of emotion like never before in this badly-written role, in this unintelligent film.

Or Carla White dreams of being Alessandra Lucenti, pictures her on set in the scene with the husband who covers his face with his hands and sobs quietly as she confesses to her monstrous infidelities, her epic fornications.

Or simply this: the celebrated actress resting between takes, playing chess with her co-star. White to mate black in three moves.

The director's voice once more: "And cut!"

Feline

You can hear her purring in the darkness, gentle engine rumble of taut cathood. Slick tail, a fan of whiskers, hot lithe creature; you'll never catch her.

Slipping in and out of bad dreams, the sorceress's familiar, female of a thousand names. Or in the midday heat, a single frame barely perceived in the lacklustre movie playing before your eyes. Either way, a disturbance, a drop of black ink in still water.

She yawns and stretches out a paw towards you. Mesmerised by eyes and claws. The flickering lights bring hard forms in and out of the picture: a dusty lampshade, piles of books, an open door. Echoes of a crime scene. You remember the murdered woman and the spiral staircase where it all began. She arches her back and grins at you. Barely there, almost invisible. Sharp little teeth glint in the sporadic light.

These literary phantoms bore me and I close the book, letting it fall to the floor.

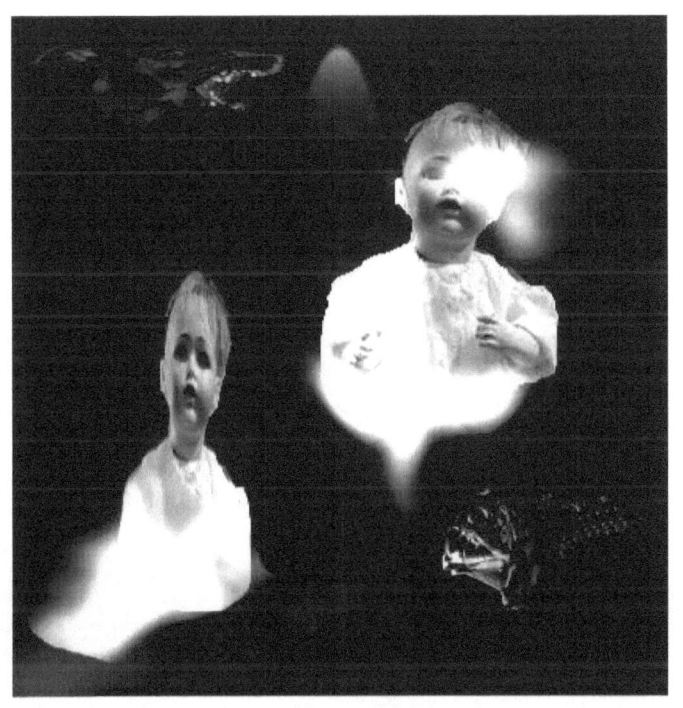

The Devil's Mirror

Pictorial III

She strobes in and out of view. Dollybird in a dark dream. White flashes, colour gone. Show us a bit more now love. Practised hands pull the top up and over her head. Hair shaken loose, snap snap snap. Black bra against skin like porcelain. Eyes widen, lips pout. Kissing whoever is watching. Mock innocence, finger to mouth, looking up at the lens. From outside in the street thunder rumbles and a car alarm sounds. Flash flash. Little drops of eternity. Pretend we're having a conversation, just talk to me about something, anything, it doesn't matter, preferably something you enjoy, a hobby maybe, just talk, I might ask the odd question, you'll look great, so natural. An arched eyebrow, a half-smile. Body segmented by the banisters. The shutter's wink, a lightning tic. Up onto the next landing and she's more feline. Down on all fours now. The total predator. Seriously darling, chat to me about just stuff, whatever, you'll look fantastic. Skirt up, showing panties and thighs, looking back at him, teasingly. Torrential rain on the windows, the car alarm's plaintive ululation. Flash flash flash flash flash flash. A rising heartbeat, shaky hands. You can say anything, tell me about your pets, you've got dogs haven't you. The catlady smirks. Then she opens her red red mouth and begins to speak. He closes his eyes and sees her in blue on white.

The Sleep of Reason

Back to the beginning again, the preparatory sketches, the makeup session that changes Alessandra Lucenti into Candice White. An incredible transformation, all agree. The perfect features of the woman whose face is the symbol of L'Oréal, Hollywood and midnight sophistication, become by infinitesimal degrees those of Britain's most notorious child killer. Hours of slow magic. Witchcraft of blusher and mascara. Dark hair turns to pitch, dreamy eyes become bored and indifferent. Full lips contract with the reflex of a sneer. Every day for two months, this subtle labour and dawn birth of the celebrated monster.

Here again, looking into the mirror, not of this world.

She reads again the note the director slipped under her door. His love is not what he claims. He is a predator, a shark. She remembers the brawl at the premiere party two years ago. Her twin sister's shocked expression. His drunken hands making threatening gestures. Showers of insults and glass. A smashed beer bottle thrust into his face, permanently scarring his left cheek. He does not know what love is; he has a nerve burdening her with such claims. She needs to focus on her character. Absently, she lets the note fall to the floor.

Cut to the scene in which he wins the right to sleep with her sister by beating her in a game of chess.

Candice White sleeps soundly in her cell. In this dream she is the celebrated femme fatale played by Alessandra Lucenti in *The Masque Ball.* A chequered ballroom floor, predators in gold masks. She is the bird queen, perfumed and smooth in a blaze of red feathers, her beak held high as she steps and whirls. There is nothing more beautiful.

Sketching out some ideas for a novel or perhaps a film, about a woman whose pathological addiction to impersonating others gets her into big trouble.

Back to the makeup session, our starting point, her starting point, the process by which she becomes somebody. It takes only the slightest changes to transmogrify her glacial beauty into something earthy, bloody and frightening. She gazes into the mirror; bored or transfixed, no-one knows.

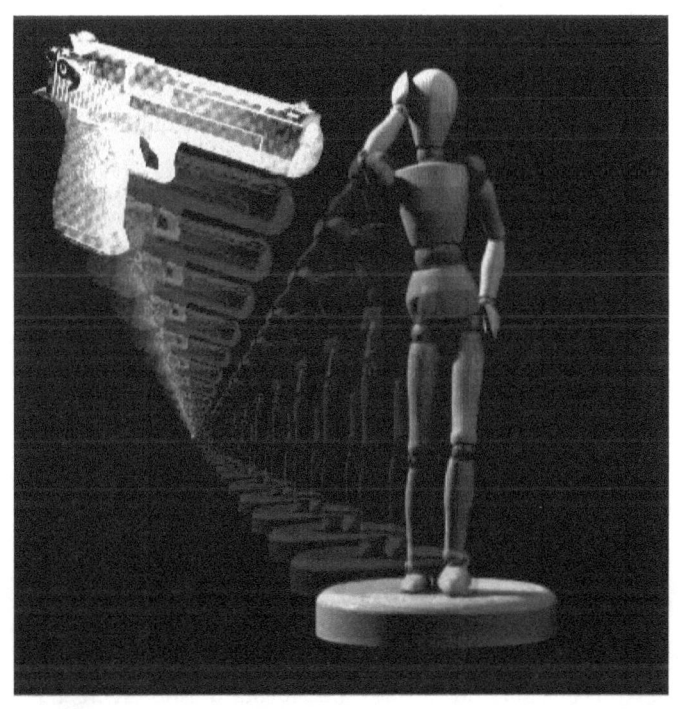

They Get What They Want

Looking Glass

My eyes itch. A metallic taste in my mouth. Every night these bad wet dreams: suffocation amidst fleshy images then waking up as I come.

What do I see? A city under rain. Rats and cockroaches in the secret places of dank neon nightclubs. A girl dancing naked under strobe lights, her torso a Morse code in the eyes of men watching hungrily from the shadows. In a dusty backroom full of lumber two identical women play a game of chess. I approach a gilt-framed mirror but it doesn't show my reflection.

I feel as if I barely exist.

Yesterday afternoon I tried to take my mind off things by watching pornos. In *Sinderella* the heroine had a threesome with her stepsisters, then went down on the handsome prince. It was shot like a music video, with hard rock playing in the background and swift cuts from one lavish set to the next. It didn't turn me on. *Masque Ball 3* was no better. In this one, Lexa Lux starred as a nymphomaniac in a ridiculous bird outfit, all plumage and tits. The predictable series of couplings left me cold, but was strangely reassuring. At least in pornography I find patterns, coherence, stability.

I get out of bed and go to the window. I stare out at the nocturnal city. Blur of lights, solitary walkers, rain.

Always this: the world, then the sheet of glass, then me.

Clone Scene

A glowing cigarette stub is flicked to the floor and the director's voice is heard, above the hubbub on set, saying, "Alright, quiet everyone, please!" A tired hand absently traces the line of the scar on his left cheek as he waits for silence. Alessandra Lucenti, in a grey trousersuit and with her hair tied back, tries to get into character. Always the most difficult part. Black words on crumpled white paper, skeletal dialogue. You have to imagine more than the scriptwriter can express. She pictures this Carla White, a version of herself, tries to look into her heart. Disconnected scenes, shot out of sequence; a story about love and murder; lines recited, perfectly inflected, but empty. Carla White is made up of glamorous nothings, a tailor's dummy for set-pieces in ballrooms and cocktail bars.

"Action!"

Playing the doctor, the director motions for Ms White to take a seat. Camera two pans over the set, taking in the doctor, his desk, a low table laden with a vase of flowers, a closed door and Carla, who sits tensely on the edge of a wicker chair. She is anxious for good news, so she must not look relaxed here; her face must wear a tight smile and she must lean towards the doctor as he recites his lines. Cameras three and four move in.

Cut to Alessandra Lucenti, naked, dreaming. Rapid eye movement over a screen showing clockwork Carla, slowly winding down.

"Stay where you are for a moment. I have something to show you." He crosses the room and opens the door, to reveal a dark-haired little girl, about six years old, in a grey skirt and t-shirt. "This is Candice. Say hello, Candice." The girl says nothing, stares vacantly ahead, as if these people, this room, this set, this story do not exist. He takes her hand and walks her over to Carla. Blank eyes stare up at her. "Now be good, Candice. This is your mummy. Say, 'Hello, mummy.'"

The girl is Alessandra Lucenti's niece and was chosen for her remarkable resemblance to the famous actress.

"Aren't you going to say hello?"

Carla White, face-to-face with her own clone. A volley of lines follows, the doctor and Carla enthusing about the miracle of science. Camera one stays fixed on the silent, motionless little girl.

Cut to Alessandra Lucenti swimming across a black lake, under livid metallic skies.

"Off you go now, that's a good girl. You can see mummy again later." There's something wrong with taciturn little Candice. She never blinks. The director imagines dissonant string music as she leaves the room and camera four captures Alessandra's faultless expression of wonder and apprehension. In scene thirty-eight (filmed yesterday) Candice will try to kill Carla, by stabbing her in the chest with a kitchen knife.

The director strokes the scar on his left cheek. "Thank you. Same time tomorrow, please."

Insomnia

The Alessandra Lucenti lookalike dances to tinny music in a glass cage. Her admirers, on the other side of the glass, form a circle of balding heads and bad suits. The lights flash red and blue. Cindy shakes her dark mane and lets her bra slip to the floor. It could be the great film star herself in there, fresh off the set of *The Masque Ball* or *Accursed*. Her ironic smile seems to say, "Maybe I am Alessandra Lucenti and this is just another role for me."

It's nearly four a.m. The night is endless. I can hear the couple in the flat below making love. Everything is too real in the metallic light that has already begun to cut through the thin curtains. A sort of death, these frozen thoughts.

Her hips gyrating to the tinny music, the walls of glass, the voyeurs. Red lights, blue lights. The man with the scar on his cheek has a gun in his pocket. Cindy has eyes like damnation; look too close and you forget who she is and everything around you. It's too late for these wankers.

I try to fall asleep. It doesn't work. I pick up the translation of Dante's Inferno *that I've been telling everyone I'm reading. Where did I get to? I never know. I start again at the beginning:*

Midway along the journey of our life

I woke to find myself in a dark wood,
for I had wandered off from the straight path.

Always from the beginning, always just setting off. From the top please, Miss Lucenti. Cindy faking it in front of strangers in suits. Gyrating, titillating, etc. The scarred man has a gun in his pocket. This is an important detail, so try to remember it later. The lights flashing red and blue. He'll use it on himself: a peepshow suicide, what a novelty, imagine his brains dribbling down the glass while the man next to him spunks in his trousers.

The artist intends you to make a connection between violent death and orgasm. Excuse me if you've heard this before...

Cindy is beautiful, more beautiful than usual, and not just because she is naked. Maybe she's perfect.

I can't sleep.

Sweet Dreams

Pictorial IV

From outside, the lonely whine of the car alarm. Leaning forward, she pulls down her skirt. That's right just make sure you're looking at the camera while you do that. She throws her head round to look in his direction, the camera captures black hair billowing, aquatic light, the stark face of the mermaid. Lightning flashes. She slips off her bra and panties. Now let's give our subscribers what they pay for. Legs splayed, lips parted. Touching herself. Flash flash flash. One hand cupping a breast. Head lolling, eyes hard, hair following the line of an arm. Beautiful. The sound of thunder, sky torn in two. Keep going sweetheart. Flash flash. Both hands at the breasts now. Lips twitch to a smile. The hands tug at the breasts, detach them, leave them on the landing floor. His hands shake so much he can barely capture this. Then it's her left leg, yanked cleanly from the hip, tossed over the banister. Thunder masks its impact on the tiles below. She hops, pirouettes, arms extended in parody of a ballerina. His hands slip, he struggles to get her into focus. That's it, keep going darling. We're nearly there! Now lying on the floor, expertly popping out the other leg. Face turns, smiles for the camera. Flash flash flash. The head's off next, rolled with playful casualness towards the stairs. He can barely keep up. Thunder makes all the windows in the house shudder. Snap snap snap snap. Their job done, the arms separate from the torso, lie inert. He goes in for the money shot. Torso wriggles away from discarded limbs. Torso has perfect skin. He wants to kiss it but he's a pro and knows his place. As he takes his last shot the car alarm stops.

The Black Crown

First he sees her walking down the stairs, under the flickering light. Children's voices rise up from the darkness of the stairwell. Her hair is dishevelled and there is a wide ladder in her left stocking. Then she is gone.

***

It is midnight and he cannot sleep for thinking about her. He remembers the flickering light, the children's voices, the ladder in her stocking. He tries to picture other details of the scene, but to no avail. Just the light, the voices, the laddered stocking. Outside the wind moans.

***

Straightening his tie, he starts walking down the stairs. His briefcase seems lighter than usual. He feels giddy. The staircase fans out beneath him like a deck of cards. For a moment he thinks he is going to fall, so he stops and sits on a stair. He puts his briefcase on his knees and opens it, so that if anyone should pass they would assume that he has suddenly remembered some important document and is making sure he has it with him. The giddiness subsides after a couple of minutes. He closes the briefcase, stands and recommences his descent, one hand on the rail. He feels light-headed again. He stops and sits for a few minutes. Then he stands and starts walking down the stairs with his eyes closed, very slowly. This does the trick, and soon he is on the ground floor.

***

There is a woman at the office whose eyes are always half-closed in smiling dreaminess, as if she has just had a very powerful orgasm. He looks at her today with renewed interest, but her hair is blonde and the woman last night had much darker hair, he thinks. He can't remember exactly, but he is pretty sure it was black hair, rather messy. He thinks about the flickering light, the laddered stocking. The blonde is staring at him. He pictures himself fucking her. Then he turns back to his work.

***

The streets are full of people. Rain falls, heavy and cold. He decides to take a different route home tonight. Lights from shops, restaurants and cars. Walking past a clothes shop he is arrested by something he has seen out of the corner of his eye. He turns and looks at the stylised female form hailing him from behind the glass. She is slender and haughty, her right hip thrust out to the side and her eyes full of callous mirth.

***

Jenny has called round. They sit on the sofa, drinking coffee. They are just good friends. He smiles at her between sips, but she can see that he is looking straight through her.

***

Midnight. He tries masturbating. Lying on his back, he imagines encounters with some of the women he works with. Other females appear too: friends, a film star. Afterwards he doesn't feel in the least sleepy. He gets up and, without putting on a dressing gown, goes to the front door of his flat. He opens it slightly and puts his eye to the crack. The flickering light reveals, in flashes, the doors of the other flats; grimy fleur-de-lis wallpaper; the monumental staircase, descending from the storeys above and continuing its downward progress at the other end of the landing. Opening the door wider, he steps through. He listens carefully, but nothing can be heard save the rain outside. Putting his front door on the latch, he walks across the landing and down a few steps. He tries to stand exactly where he had seen her the night before. He shifts to the right, then slightly to the left. He closes his eyes. He strains to remember her exact posture, her movements. Did she touch the handrail? His mind is blank.

***

He goes for a walk in the countryside. In the middle of the valley is a hill. He takes the muddy path that winds up its side in narrow coils. At the top he sits on a vandalised bench and looks down at the panorama. Though the sun is high in a cloudless sky the mists of morning have not yet entirely dispersed. One area in particular, directly in front of him, still retains a thick screen of mist, hemmed in by trees. Beyond that, maybe three of four miles away, is the power station. He can't see the main building but surmounting the wall of mist, perched impossibly in the air, is the top section of the chimney, an enchanted tower. He tries to imagine the rest of the chimney and the building below, but the white nothingness of the mist defies his stare, refutes his conviction that something must exist to support the floating edifice. He gazes, baffled, into the haze.

***

The stairway again. He can't escape it. Everything brings him back here. He has to use the stairs to get to his flat at the end of the day, and he has to use them to go out again. The stairway connects the various parts of his life, private and social. He goes to his flat to be alone, or occasionally to entertain friends, and he leaves it to perform the various activities that keep him alive and a part of society: work, shopping, socialising. He cannot get from one area of his existence to another without entering the stairway and walking up or down those same stairs that she used

173

that night, all those weeks ago. So it isn't just the stairway he cannot get away from; it is her too. Although he has seen her only once, briefly and from behind, she is a constant presence on the stairs. He cannot do anything without brushing past her phantom.

***

He can barely manage three mouthfuls of food. He eyes his chicken breast balefully. The pores of its skin are craters in a sickly landscape, the dark sauce a quagmire. Jenny has finished her helping. She automatically scoops his chicken onto her own plate and begins taking great mouthfuls, her knife and fork cutting and shining like infernal machinery. Half an hour later he is bent double over the lavatory bowl, belching up his emptiness. She stands on the other side of the bathroom door, biting her lower lip. Her hand rests on the door handle, but she doesn't go in.

***

He dreams her. She is walking naked across the open-plan office, oblivious to everyone around her. She has the eyes of a corpse. Eventually she reaches the top of the spiral staircase. Fingers with nails the colour of blood stroke the handrail. She seems to be descending, though her feet are not moving. He runs so fast to catch her that he stumbles and falls tumbling down the stairs, bouncing horribly, his bones cracking

174

with every impact, until he lies at the bottom of the staircase, a broken doll, neck twisted, arms convulsed, eyes empty.

***

In the night he is awoken by the sound of children laughing outside his front door. None of this is real, he tells himself. But he cannot go back to sleep. He stares at the ceiling until the first stirrings of dawn.

Amnesia

Notes on the texts and dates of composition

Most of the texts in this volume have appeared online.

Phantoms

Beginnings I, II & III, The Beach, The Carcass, The Corpse 1998-9. Originally part of a longer sequence, *The Birth of Venus*. **The Corpse** was revised in 2007.

Golgotha 2002. Originally intended as part of *Labyrinth*, an interactive web-based installation.

At Night the Mannequins Play Dead 2004.

Tramp 1995. A version of this poem appeared in *Oasis 77*, March 1996.

Brassaï in Paris 2001.

Vampire 1994. A version of this poem appeared in *Odyssey*, Autumn 1996.

Moth 2003.

Homage to Pierre Reverdy 1994. Published in *Blue Cage* 4, Spring 1995.

The Song of the Clowns 2001. Revised 2004.

Mad Uncle 1995.

Girls Outside a London Nightclub 1994. Minor revisions 2007.

Landscape with Bones 1994. Published in *Oasis 77*, March 1996.

~~ground zero~~ 2003.

Lava

Rant 2005.

Body 2001.

Bells Shatter... 2004.

Nightmares 2004.

Improvisations 1, 12 & 15 2001.

Mirror

Daddy Short-legs 2004.

First Sadness 2004.

Lights Out 2002. Originally intended as part of *Labyrinth*, an interactive web-based installation.

[ink] 2004.

Blood 2002. Originally coupled with the picture *The Musician's Pact* [see page 5].

Worm 2001.

Me-Poems 2001. Number two published on http://www.niederngasse.com, with various artworks.

Reflections 1995. Published in *Terrible Work* 7, 1997.

A Beach 1993.

Contraptions

The Day Angels Took Over the Machines 1996.

Only a Matter of Time... 1996.

An Expert in His Field Examines an Antique Machine 1994. Published in *Terrible Work* 7, 1997.

Nude Falling Down a Staircase Both poems composed 2001.

First Principles 2006.

René & Renée

All texts composed 2000, except:

Escape & The Bad Leg 1999.

Metamorphosis 2002.

Coming of Age 2001.

The Small Hours

All of the texts and images in this section were originally part of *Labyrinth*, an interactive web-based installation.

All texts composed 2003-4, except:

Pictorial IV 2006.